MIDNIGHT
STORM
MOONLESS
SKY

Also By Alex Soop

Whistle At Night and They Will Come
Indigenous Horror Stories, Volume 2

MIDNIGHT STORM MOONLESS SKY

INDIGENOUS HORROR STORIES

ALEX SOOP

Illustrations: Patricia Soop & Alex Soop

DURVILE &
UpRoute Books

Calgary, Alberta, Canada

DURVILE.COM

DURVILE &
UpRoute Books

UpRoute Imprint of Durvile Publications Ltd.
Calgary, Alberta, Canada
www.durvile.com

Copyright © 2022 Alex Soop

Library and Archives Cataloguing in Publications Data

MIDNIGHT STORM MOONLESS SKY
INDIGENOUS HORROR STORIES

Soop, Alex; Author
Soop, Patricia; Illustrations
Soop, Alex; Illustrations
Bell, Jillian; Editor

1. First Nations | 2. Blackfoot | 3. Indigenous | 4. Supernatural | 5. Paranormal

The UpRoute "Spirit of Nature" Series
Series Editors, Raymond Yakeleya and Lorene Shyba

Issued in print and electronic formats
ISBN: 978-1-990735-12-7 (pbk); 978-1-990735-21-9 (e-pub)
978-1-990735-18-9 (audiobook)

Front cover design, Austin Andrews
Back cover photograph, Dima Gulpa
Book design, Lorene Shyba

The lands where studios stand are a part of the ancient homeland and traditional territory of many Indigenous Nations, as places of hunting, travel, trade, and healing. The Treaty 7 Peoples of Southern Alberta include the Siksika, Piikani, and Kainai of the Niisitapi (Blackfoot) Confederacy; the Dene Tsuut'ina; and the Chiniki, Bearspaw, and Wesley Stoney Nakoda First Nations. We also acknowledge the homeland of the Métis Nation of Alberta. We honour the Nations and Peoples, as well as the land. We commit to serving the needs of Indigenous Peoples today and into the future.

Durvile Publications would like to acknowledge the financial support of the Government of Canada through Canadian Heritage Canada Book Fund and the Government of Alberta, Alberta Media Fund.

Canada   Alberta
Government

DEDICATION

For Darby and Philly,
two late brothers who always
backed up my never-ending love for the arts.

CONTENTS

BRINGING ABOUT
A DIFFERENT MEANING

WHAT'S A HORROR STORY? Well first things first: let's start with the label, shall we? Horror.

When I hear this word, I envision a whole whack of slasher movies—the iconic, antagonistic killer kind. I grew up on slasher films; the original terrors that kicked off my eternal love for the genre.

I remember visiting my family on the Blood Reserve, also now known as the Kainai Nation, when I was about five or six. My teenage uncle was often in charge and rather than entertain us kids himself, he would put some old horror movie on the VHS. I was exposed to the world of monsters and ghouls at an age when I should have been worrying about when Santa was coming.

My first real taste of the oral kind of horror storytelling was when I was sent to live with my grandparents on the rez. Living with my Papa and Gramma was my Papa's brother, Everett Soop. He was a well-known artist and political satire cartoonist, but to me he was Uncle Buno. One real knack he had, besides his own writing and drawing skills, was his ability to concoct the wildest tales of terror.

You see, my grandparents just happened to live in the vicinity of one of two of the Blood Reserve's old residential schools. St. Paul's, the one we lived by, had been abandoned for close to twenty years and had fallen into a state of total disrepair. My friends and I would sometimes brave up and go exploring this creepy old place— risking a spanking if we were caught.

St. Paul's Indian Residential School was often where Uncle Buno would go to when he needed a spooky setting for one of his spine-tingling stories. Following the telling of one of his stories, I would sit there with Buno in the kitchen, Gramma and Papa having gone out on errands. The construction of our house stretched back to the 1930s, around the same time as the abandoned residential schools, and I'd be scared out of my wits, jumping at the slightest sound of the old house creaking and groaning. The entire southwestern area of the reserve felt like one big setting for *The Twilight Zone*. I became enthralled and terrified of the paranormal world.

Uncle Buno was not the only relative on the rez to teach me the craft of storytelling. We Blackfoot tend to be very close to our blood relations. I had numerous cousins and aunts and uncles who had a knack for giving us kids the fright of our lives as we sat around a campfire. So therefore, with so much of my young life under the spell of creepy tales of terror, it was no wonder I picked up the pen (or keyboard) to dive into my own world of horror stories; Indigenous horror that is.

Indigenous storytelling goes back at least a millennium. Quite often myths and legends were concocted to scare the wits out of the kids so they wouldn't stray away from the camp at night and encounter the real horrors of life. Imagine the horror of a bear attack, or a wild pack of hungry wolves, or even big wildcats.

But horror isn't just the world of paranormal ghosts and demons. To many others, horror may bring about a whole different meaning in life. Everyday situations can be anyone's horror story—real-life scenarios like a lone woman being stalked through a darkened back alley; a merciless case of road rage gone terribly wrong; worrying about a teenage daughter while she's out on her first date; getting lost while out on a hike, and so on. Anything can happen in everyday life, and quite often they can be a whole new-fangled tale of horror on their own. So, in the following pages, I have concocted my own scenarios and eerie tales which I hope will keep you up at night. Enjoy, my loyal readers.

—Alex Soop, 2022

~ ONE ~

AN UNLIKELY
TURN OF EVENTS

COURT ORDERED OR NOT, I don't know why I still come to these stupid meetings. Maybe it's my conscience wanting to do my mom's bidding. I have been free, sober, and clean of alcohol for well over three years, and there's no way in hell I'm going back to that lonely, despair-riddled life. A prison stint and losing my young marriage to divorce was more than enough to wake me up from the devastating effects of the devil's nectar. Although every time I think of my ex taking the house, my car, and the dog—the damn dog—I want to slam back a bottle or two. But I don't. Living three years without the stuff was what I really needed to realize that I didn't need it in my life any more than I do coca-cola or chocolate cake.

The sudden wave of polite clapping pulls my head from the clouds, and my mind rushes back to the world of this dimly lit, stale-smelling church basement.

"Thank you, Riley," says Trina, this AA assembly's chairperson. "Now, would anyone else care to take the podium?" Sitting comfortably at the head of the room, she swivels in her steel chair and glances around at the small, seated crowd of recovering alcoholics, her eyes falling and staying put on me. I look away for a few seconds to admire a painted picture of a stoic-looking Jesus, then glance back to see Trina still gleaming at me, smiling.

"How about you ... Paul, was it?" she says.

"Yeah," I say, tonelessly. "My name is Paul."

"You're still relatively new here? You've been here a few times, and I don't believe we've heard you speak yet. Would you care to get up and tell us a little bit about yourself?" she asks. She sounds sweet and makes me think of my late aunty, Delores. Trina even shares my late aunt's hairstyle.

I watched my grandfather drink himself practically to death. Those were the final years of my high school days and the kickoff to my own days of drinkin' hard.

I'd much rather be that guy who just sits in without saying a peep, nodding in accordance whenever someone's story hits a soft spot. "Sure," I say, "why not." The wave of dainty clapping resumes as I get off my stiff seat and move through the centre aisle of foldable steel chairs, the musty smell getting stronger as I approach the makeshift stage. A heavy plume of heat sprays down on me from a ceiling vent.

Standing behind the rickety lectern, I survey the small crowd. A tall guy in the back wearing a grey Stetson stares lecherously at a pretty blonde with her back to him, her ponytail adding a sense of boredom. An old couple sit with one another, holding each other's hands as they stare up at me like two cats watching a mouse stroll across the room. Trina sits on the very left of the front row. She stares at me as if to say go on, we're here to listen.

Finally I notice a tall, lanky man slumping in his chair, his long legs messily strewn on the floor in front of him. His attention switches back and forth from me to a beautiful woman sitting two chairs from him who is doing her level best to ignore him. I steer my eyes clear of this pretty woman in fear of losing my cool before I share my less-than-luminous history.

"Hi, uh,"—I clear my throat—"hello, my name is Paul—"

A small babble of hellos, with my name added in, surges throughout the eight attendees.

"—I am—was an alcoholic. I uhh,"—eyes darting—"well, my life story is a pretty long one, so I'll try and keep it short and simple. Alcoholism has run rampant throughout my family stemming back a few generations. I watched my grandfather, who raised me to the best of his good knowledge, drink himself practically to death. Those were the final years of my high school days and the kickoff to my own days of drinkin' hard. My grandfather initiated his own life of alcoholism due to his tours of duty in the Vietnam War, and way before that, the Canadian residential school system—"

When I mention residential school, I hear the guy with the long legs scoff and snort. I stop talking and shoot an unkind glare at him as he squirms to get comfortable in his seat. His spiteful grin suggests his own life story of being brought up by racists.

"Terry," Trina barks. "You know the rule of cross-talk." She waits until Terry composes himself and is once again paying attention to me, his lips sealed. She reverts back to her sweetness, encouraging me silently with her glance that, once again, reminds me of my aunt.

"Uh, as I was saying, my grandfather suffered many abuses in residential school, effects that never really wore off, I guess you could say. So, he was only able to find his coping mechanisms at the bottom of the bottle, and as a young kid, I watched—"

Shuffling his long legs around, Terry once again lets out a scoff.

I am about to blow up like a hand grenade, but Trina beats me to it. She bolts from her chair to face the disruption. "Excuse me, Terry. Do you want to be a part of this meeting, or would you rather be off and out?"

I cut in, saying, "No, wait, hold on, Trina. Maybe he has something important to say. Let's just hear him out, if you don't mind?"

She turns to face me, still reeling in frustration, and nods once. "If that's what you'd like, then I'm all ears." She sits back down in her squeaky chair and folds her arms.

"Go ahead, Terry. Let me hear what's on your mind," I say, discharging my pent-up frustration by squeezing onto the edges of the lectern.

"Do I stand or sit? You know what, never mind," Terry says. "I just gotta say this: the residential school system depravity you speak of, its absolute bullsh—BS." In the dim 60-watt light bulb illumination, I could clearly see that he is of the discriminatory sort of white guy, with greasy, split hair ends peeking out at all angles from the back of his beat-up trucker's cap. Storybook redneck. "If anything, it was what the damn Indians needed. What with them living their savage ways of life and all. I, for one, agree with our country's past and the way it dealt with the damn savages. And that's just—"

"Excuse me!" Trina snaps, leaping to her feet once more. She glares at Terry. "This isn't a debate club. And even if it was, your racist views would not be welcome here, especially in this House of God."

House of God. It's my turn to scoff, only I keep it to myself. I am standing in the basement of a church of the same religion that helped develop the North American residential school system. I shake off my wandering notion and reapply my attention to the riled-up Trina, putting into practice the best tool from my prison days to avoid trouble:

Walk away and be the better man.

"As a matter of fact, as the chairperson of this evening's AA, I would very much like to ask you to leave," orders Trina. This time, the applause has more spirit. Terry doesn't hesitate. He leaps from his seated position, nearly knocking the creaky chair to the floor, and storms out of the basement chamber, releasing a fusillade of foul language in his brash, swaggering wake.

Trina remains standing until we hear the hindmost basement door slam shut. She relocates her consideration to me and says, "I'm so sorry about that, Paul. Please, carry on with what you were saying." I realize I've said all I need to say.

Trina is the type to take the time to stop at a doughnut shop and purchase premium coffee and doughnuts for the meeting attendees out of her own pocket. I always wait until the end of the meeting to grab some of her coffee; drinking it during a meeting makes me overly warm and fidgety when I'm trying to sit and listen to the AA assembly's stories. The coffee warms my blood for my short walk back to my home, though. Coffee in one hand and a half-eaten doughnut in the other, I'm ready to head to the coat rack when I feel a sprightly tap to my shoulder blade. I choke down my chunk of half-chewed doughnut and face my not-so-much of a disturber.

"I was really moved by your account," says the beautiful woman who'd been sitting a couple of chairs away from racist Terry. "I'm sorry to hear about what happened to you from your days of drinking. It's good that you come to these meetings, though. And I'm especially impressed by how composed you kept yourself after hearing what that racist asshole had to say. That must have been so friggin' hard."

A stream of outright bashfulness hits me, but I manage to overcome it by curling my feet into fists inside my boots. It always helps for reasons I am unaware of. "Thank you. And most definitely, I wouldn't miss these meetings for the world. They do wonders to help me live life without alcohol." I place my coffee cup down on the table, dust off my hand and thrust it out. "I'm—"

"—Paul. Yeah, I know," she says with a smile, planting her soft hand into my palm and squeezing with construction-worker strength. "I'm Rashida."

"Rashida?" I say, wide-eyed. "Just like the actor. That's a beautiful name." Her eyes alone ripen the beauty her name carries along with it.

"Thank you, it's Turkish," she giggles, her eyes darting away from mine as her fingers twirl through her shoulder-length, almost jet-black hair shimmering in the mellow basement lighting.

An awkward moment of uncomfortable silence bloomed between us.

Not this time, I think.

"So," I blurt out, making her snap some undivided

attention back to me. "You—uhh—did you have to travel far to get here?" I ask, the first question that sails into my mind.

She lights up like Santa Claus really does exist. "Yes—and no. I live just a few blocks from the downtown core, sorta uptown if you wanna call it. My dad picks me up and drives me home from each meeting. Just to make sure I'm actually going."

"Oh, your dad? That's nice of him," I say, half-asking an unspoken question.

"Yeah." She smiles and looks down at her feet. "A typical Islamic father. He told me he'd run me out of the family if I didn't stop drinking." She looks up from her shoes. "I picked up the habit from my university friends."

"There was probably a little bit of BS in that?" I ask, pinching my fingers together at eye level. "I mean, he really wouldn't do that, would he?"

"Yeah, I think he most likely would. It's against our religion," she says. "And how about you? Travel far to get here?"

I look upward at the dust-smeared ceiling, already knowing what I'm going to say. "Not at all. I live just a few blocks from here. Just a short walk for me."

"Wow. You're so lucky. I've always wanted to have my own place in the heart of downtown."

I wince a little. "Well, it's not all the hype that I thought it would be," I say. "Rent's expensive, and the traffic sucks. And the smog and drunks—well, that's a different story on its own. I miss the good old country."

Rashida's eyes are trained on mine. It seems like she looks right through me, dropping her tense shoulders to rummage through her purse. She extracts a vibrating smartphone. "Sorry, I have to take this really quick."

"By all means." She walks off a few feet to take her call in private.

Now is the time. I consume the rest of my doughnut in haste and gulp back my coffee while it's still warm.

Within a minute, Rashida is back and standing in front of me. "Speak of the devil. That was my dad. He's outside, waiting impatiently—like always." She rolls her eyes. "I guess I'd better get going." She doesn't leave right away, almost like she's waiting for something.

Do I ask her for her number? I decide it's still too early for that level of intimacy. "Will you be here for the next meeting?"

She lights up again, "Yes."

"I'll see you then," I say, the coolness of my voice not betraying how nervous I feel. "And perhaps I can buy you a latte afterwards? I mean don't get me wrong, Trina's coffee is hella good and all, but I do like me an old-fashioned French vanilla. Made the authentic way."

"So, you know of a place around here?" she asks.

"I do."

"Okay then," she says, still beaming brightly. "I'm so down. But look, I better get going before Grumpy Grady goes all off on me. See you soon?"

I nod and smile.

"Okay. Bye," she says and waves before vanishing up the stairs, leaving me in a state of contentment. Yes. Scored a date without even having to ask for her cell-phone number.

I gather up my coat, refill my paper cup and thank Trina on a job well done.

"See you next time," Trina hollers as I ascend the small staircase leading up to the back alley.

IT'S A NICE NIGHT OUT. I settle for taking a minor detour through the city's once-upon-a-time-ago red light district. The always-busy avenue is now a sideline of lively bars and classy restaurants, some with people out on the patios. Two blocks in and I realize I've made a mistake. All the happy people swigging back glasses of beer and sparkling wine is enough to drive a devilish craving through my body.

A swift exit to the nearest back alley it is.

Much like the typical gloomy back lanes near my apartment, this one is barely lit except for a dingy neon light blinking: Monarch Bar & Grill, barely illuminating the parking lot in a wash of strobing red and yellow. I tread through the grit-speckled pavement, my peripheral vision landing on a group of men milling about in front of a closed set of steel doors. One man is half grounded. I'd seen my share of barfights and knew one when I saw it.

"Call me a camel jockey, will you, you racist piece of shit?" barks one of the men as he throws a haymaker at the man on his knees in a praying plead.

I remain motionless in the centre of the alley, watching until one of the men sees me and eyes me harshly. "You best keep walking if you know what's good for you, guy," he advises.

This isn't my fight. I heed the advice and keep on moving, strolling away until I reach a dumpster where I hide and keep on watching.

Unlike most of my family members, I was one of the lucky few. Prescription eyeglasses were never a necessity, but seeing in the dark? I'm no Andean night monkey. I stare out from my half cover of the sour-smelling dumpster, but I can't perceive shades of skin tones that might make sense of the racial slur that no doubt brought on this horrible street fight. What I can see is three hooded figures circling another guy whose face is already obscured with blood. That man, on his knees, crashes to the pavement from a swift kick that bangs out from one of the hooded figures, then another, and another. The hooded guys take turns jeering and kicking. The man on the ground rolls over and groans. At least he's not dead. In the dim light of the blinking neon sign, in spite of all the blood, I recognize the face of the man now resting on his back, no battered trucker cap in sight. It's Terry.

"Gettin' a taste of your own medicine?" I whisper under my breath, my inner voice laughing like a madman. I watch as the attackers start feeding Terry a last round of kicks to the ribs. I had, in years past, trained in martial arts and was a fan of fight movies and pay-per-view events. But the real life, no-holds-barred street fight action was too much to bear. I stand up, turn my face away, and walk away eastward to my apartment building, which stands among one of the many vertical towers in sight.

I am hardly a block from the site of the brawl—if it could even be called that—when a piercing scream curdles my blood like death on the airwaves.

Keep going. The son of a bitch deserves it, says the bad wolf side of my psyche. But then the other side feels sympathy for Terry's agonized shrieks of agony.

The wolves' voices in my head are replaced with my Gramma's voice: "Would you want the same for you? What if a man walked by while you were getting jumped by a group of men, and just kept on strolling like his shit don't stink?" Even her stout, charming face comes to mind.

"Fine," I say out loud. I turn back and head toward

the commotion. Maybe some calming words might stop the guys from going further with the beat down.

By the time I reach the dispute, all three men are throwing in their own mixture of kicks and punches at the limp body on the pavement.

"Guys," I interrupt.

Nothing.

"Guys!" I belt.

Three heads whip around and face me, eyes flashing with hate.

"He looks like he's had enough." I point at Terry, his body twisted as he moans in pain, his face covered in streaks of crimson.

"I thought I told you to keep walking," says one of the men, his hair styled into a slicked-back pompadour. "Just don't know when to mind your own business, eh?"

"Yeah," says the other. He glances down at the writhing body on the street, then stares back at me. "I guess you're a part of this now. Come on, fellas." He struts toward me, the remaining two toughs hard on his heels like a roving hyena pack moving in for the kill.

"Oh shit," I whisper to myself, backtracking on the heels of my boots.

"Now you've gone and done it, dummy," utters Gramma's raspy voice in my head. "I would have called the police or gotten help, not try to go all Bruce Lee on them."

Speaking of Bruce Lee, I am about to find out how handy my acquired fighting skills come in. See if the action movies were really what they seemed when one man takes on three and wins.

It isn't.

Of course not.

My vision immediately goes black for a split second,

while at the same time, my eardrums thump like the time I crashed my mountain bike. I remember how much that one hurt; my collar bone snapped in two places.

My vision returns. I'm still standing. Muscle memory kicks in, and I swing for the first face in sight. One of the guys goes down right away. I smile and decree a mini, muted celebration until I feel a hundred bee stings to my right torso. I turn again to catch the next guy, grinning viciously, looking pretty pleased with himself. The switchblade he holds in his hand is dripping with blood. My blood ....

"You mother—" This time, I use my feet, winding up a roundhouse kick. The kick lands square in his chest, the impact sending the switchblade flying from his hands. I don't have time to celebrate before the next hooded guy comes at me.

I know what comes next.

All I can do is cover my face. I try to protect it so I don't look too battered up for my first, off-the-record date with Rashida. Her smiling face tears away from my mind as the blows commence. One after the other. Each one more painful than the last. Finally, my body has enough. It shuts down like a powered-up laptop thrown out the window onto a sidewalk ten floors below.

STILL STARRY, my vision returns like a black hole in reverse. The repetitive beep of a monitor accompanies the chemical scent of hospital air.

Too many movies have portrayed what I'm currently feeling. The Bruce Lee scenes may have been overly bogus, but Hollywood got one part right: the unforeseen wake-up in the uncomfortable and humiliating confines of a hospital bed. At least all these brutal bruises and searing pains haven't totally killed me off yet, they've been stalled by the medley of painkillers flowing through my bloodstream.

My neck still hurts. I ignore the searing pain to face the window, the silhouette sitting against the ambient light still not fully in focus. The figure stands up and approaches my side.

I only recognize the voice.

"I'm so, so sorry for what I said to you the other night," he moans. In this most unlikely turn of events, I recognize Terry's voice. "You—you saved my life, man."

TWO

THE WAIL OF
THE WIND

PART I

"Sorry, Mr. Injun, but no can do. I can only offer ya's the four strips of smoked moose meat for your two beaver pelts."

"My name is Jackson, not Injun," declared the man standing before the fur trader.

The trader shrugged. "Whatever ya say. My offer's the same. You can take it or leave it."

As Jackson contemplated this offer, he noticed the blank, staring gaze of a wolf head hanging on the wall behind the merchant counter. The wolf's energy was frozen in a state of defence, an aggressive snarl revealing snow-white teeth which gleamed in the dim, fire-lit room.

"That's the absolute best you can do?" he asked without averting his mesmerized gaze from the wolf's glassy stare.

The trader shrugged as he made his lame excuse. "It's been real bad for us these past few months. I'll tell you that much. The game just ain't comin' along here like they used to do."

Jackson studied the trader and his long-arched, hawk nose that protruded beneath his thin wireframe spectacles. His bushy handlebar mustache brushed over the top of brown, tobacco-dripping lips. A recent haircut was the only decent attribute to the man's otherwise disheveled appearance.

"Okay then," Jackson huffed. "I guess we will have to take it." He whirled around and summoned his son, Jed, who was busy wandering around the small cabin, gazing in awe at the trophy kills of stuffed animals and head pieces hanging on the walls.

"Son, come, and bring the beaver pelts."

Jed scurried over and looked up at his father with big, round eyes. He handed over the buckskin pack he had slung over his slender shoulders. Jackson grasped the bag with both hands and overturned it, spilling out the contents: two freshly cleaned beaver pelts.

The fur trader's eyes lit up at the sight of the prized beaver skins with their soft auburn fur. He flashed a broken smile of half-rotted teeth, browned from years of neglect and chewing tobacco. "Damn, them is some hella good lookin' furs. I reckon ya just got 'em cleaned didja?" Jackson nodded half-heartedly. It was an inequitable exchange but his family needed food. The long winter at hand had no end in sight.

Snatching the beaver pelts for a closer examination, the fur trader tossed them in a darkened corner behind the exchange counter. "I'll just be a quick moment. You two gentlemen jus' sit tight now. Hell, y'oughta have a look around." The man looked down and winked at Jed before turning to exit the room. He spewed a sickly fluid into a rusted spittoon at the foot of the counter and vanished into the back room through a makeshift door of an unknown, tattered fabric.

"Pa, we aren't trading two whole pelts for but only four strips of meat, are we?" Jed asked in Anishinaabe.

Jackson's attention was back on the wolf head hanging on the wall behind the counter. *A wolf on a wall is a tragic insult to its spirit,* he thought to himself. His train of thought sunk deeply in the blank, dead gaze of this grey and white wolf, its glossy marble eyes reflecting the dancing red from the room's corner fireplace. He was reminded of a similar winter's night when he'd been much younger and had crossed paths with such a wolf as this—a momentous turning point in his life. He had gone adrift from his cousin while they were out on their first solo hunting voyage. They were twelve years old, and Jackson's own papa, Jed's granddad, had felt it was time for he and his cousin to learn to hunt on their own.

JACKSON AND HIS FAVORITE COUSIN had finished resetting their fruitless trap lines, and set out, chancing upon an array of bloody hoof-like tracks in the snow. They followed the tracks for a short time, when a sudden and unexpected blizzard enshrouded the land in a whiteout of blustering flurries. The blinding squall pelted snow sideways, and the bitter chill ravaged the exposed, delicate skin of Jackson's young face. To his good fortune, one of his earlier traps he'd set had snared a plump rabbit, which he stowed away in his pack.

With his head bowed to partly shield himself from the deadly wind, he hadn't realized he and his cousin, unlikely to hear each other in the howling storm, had trailed off in separate directions. Instead of panicking, Jackson kept his head low with his rifle slung over his shoulder and trudged firmly head-on against the piercing wind. He was dressed well for the weather and knew the end of the storm's onslaught would come sooner if he walked into the heart of it rather than stay put or go with the stream of the winds. He knew his cousin would surely be doing the same.

Through the relentless spray of ice and snow, he trudged for hours on end, thinking that the storm would never tire. At last, he came to a dead end; he looked up and realized he was at the bottom end of a massive rock face. The vertical rise extended up further than he could see through the swirling snow.

The storm amplified again, the wind wailing through the trees like a pack of angry wolves. He gathered as much wood as he needed to get him through the night.

Exhausted, the cold finally biting through the layers of his clothing, he scaled along the base of the cliff, the cliff face itself being his guide.

The storm abated somewhat, and he came upon the mouth of a darkened cave opening. He eyed the ceiling of shifting clouds. The sun was beginning to hide behind the sky-scraping evergreen horizon, so he decided he would set up camp and spend the night in the dark and vacant cave.

Putting into play his newly acquired outdoors-man skills, Jackson built a small fire, using up the loose twigs scattered on the floor of the cave. Once the fire was ignited enough to blaze on its own, he went about in search of more wood to burn from the skeletal trees just outside the cave. As he stepped outside, the storm amplified again, the wind wailing and howling through the trees like a pack of angry wolves. Jackson shuddered. He gathered as much wood as he thought needed to get him through the night and hastily returned inside with an armful of fallen twigs and thick branches. His grey woolen jacket was caked in white.

He felt blessed; at least he had food for the night.

Jackson removed a half-frozen carcass from his pack and carefully skinned the rabbit, just as his father had taught him. The razor-sharp knife slid through the outer layer of fat like warm butter. He peeled back the skin, revealing tender white and pink sinewy muscles. The potent, coppery smell of blood was masked by the infusion of cool wintery draft and wafting fire smoke hanging heavy in the interior of the cave. Slicing his knife upward toward the neck, he raised the thick skin off the back, gripped hard with his blood-covered hands, and grunted loudly as he snapped the rabbit's neck, tearing the head clean from the body. Gently he placed the head on the ground, facing the lifeless staring eyes away from him.

His pa had told him to never let any part of an animal's body go to waste for fear of a swift vengeance by its spirit. He would later say a prayer for the rabbit and bury the head once he was done preparing the rest of the body for traditional use and consumption.

Jackson ate until his stomach felt full, while the smell of cooked meat wafted through the frosty, stagnant air of the cave. He stored the leftovers of the rabbit meat inside a sack made from the stomach lining of a moose. The rest of the rabbit meat would have to suffice for breakfast before he was to move out at the break of dawn.

Following the small, portioned meal and the long strenuous hours of the snowy day's trekking through the blizzard, sleep came fast. In no time, he plunged into a heavy slumber, lying alongside the rhythmic crackling of the dancing fire.

He dreamt he was in a midnight blizzard, standing in an open, treeless field, alone, scarcely clothed, and defenceless. All around him was an infinity of pallor, like a white universe devoid of moon or stars. The snow was whipping violently sideways, downwards, and even upwards from the ground.

Jackson pressed forward until, at last, he saw a lone tree in the distance, standing tall like a giant with a great head of sprouting hair. He dashed for it, hoping there would be some refuge from the gnawing hunger of snow and wind.

He reached the tree. It was enormous, with a trunk as dense as a wigwam base. He stalked the exterior of smooth rounded bark until he came to a large opening. His half-naked body easily slipped inside. To his surprise, it was warm inside. He huddled motionless, trying to keep himself inside, warm against the elements. Then the wind picked up again and shook the thick tree trunk side to side with Jackson tucked inside its bowels. Howling like an enormous wolf, the wind became so deafening that he had to shield his ears with his hands, and still, it screamed at him.

Back in the cave, Jackson awoke with a start. His heart raced, and his breathing came in forced gasps. The howling wind from his dream was still fresh in his mind. He shivered, but not from the cold. He had heard wolves many times before, but this dream howling was like a beast of immense magnitude, anguished from insatiable hunger pains.

The fire had died down to a few burning red embers, but a faint light already glistened through the entrance of the cave—morning daylight. Jackson's heart slowed, and he breathed normally for the first time since he'd woken. He made the decision to venture back outside to gather more wood to cook the leftover rabbit meat.

As soon as he rose to his feet, the howling returned. It was as clear as the daylight seeping in. He clutched the lapels of his coat and squeezed tight until his knuckles turned white. This howling, however, was unlike the sound from his dream. It drifted through the cavernous air like a child's ghostly weeping, emanating from deep within the cave. Jackson was ready to bolt when the howl came again, sounding more like a dog's wail.

A wolf's wail.

Wolves and caves often meant pups. Which in turn meant danger—an angered mother wolf's danger.

He grabbed his rifle from the ground and pointed it down the dark, jagged funnel toward the tail-end of the cave. He had unknowingly stepped right into a wolf's den. He knew very well that his single-shot rifle would do very little against an angry pack of disturbed wolves.

With his rifle pointed at the darkness, he stepped back a few feet and kicked at the nearly fire, stirring up the embers until they glowed bright red. In the glow of the embers, he saw the illuminated reflection of canine eyes glowing in the short distance from the flare up of the disturbed embers.

Only one set of eyes.

Jackson exhaled a breath of relief, keeping his rifle aimed at the glowing eyes. It seemed like he stood motionless with his rifle at the ready for hours. He held his rifle at shoulder until his arms began to feel like boulders.

Finally, feeling neither man nor beast was about to make the first move, he gently let his rifle drop to the ground so that he could rest his aching arms. Staring hard, he kept his vigilant attention fixed straight ahead of him until his own vision adjusted to the darkness creeping in around him.

The light from outside finally seeped in, and Jackson could make out the rough texture of the walls of the cave where he'd taken shelter. The walls rippled, and the floor was worn down like ancient bedrock, smoother than he had originally thought. The roof couldn't have been more than ten feet high, just enough for him to move about without impaling himself on one of the many down-pointed projections of spike-tipped rock stakes.

Jackson was uncertain if it was only the one wolf all alone in the den or a sleeping pack in the farthest reaches.

He wasn't about to linger to find out. Hastily and silently, he gathered his belongings and skulked toward the mouth of the cave. The storm outside had dissipated; the daylight blinded him temporarily as though he was entering through the pearly white gates.

His boots crunched in the fresh blanket of snow as he made his retreat. He made sure he was well clear of the overhang of the outer cave before he threw a curious glance over his shoulder.

There, the wolf pup rested on its tailbone, watching him curiously.

Jackson stopped and whirled around to face the wolf pup head-on. It was small, white, and ashen with a bright pink nose, and it yawned widely and stared back at Jackson with soft eyes.

Jackson turned to run, but something held him back. He thought for a moment, then turned again and

He stopped and whirled around to face the wolf pup head-on.
The wolf waited, watching him curiously.

headed back for the cave opening. The wolf pup, seeing Jackson's approach, rose to all fours and scampered
back inside the cave.

His inner-most conscience questioned why he was
going back inside, not knowing what kind of fate awaited
him on arrival. He knew all too well that a mother wolf,
much less an entire pack, would defend their young at
any cost. Still, he ventured in.

The embers of his onetime firepit were now just a
pile of smouldering ashes. The rabbit head was gone.

His vision, attuned to the blinding glare of the sun
and snow outside, left him nearly blind once again. He

crept in and stopped near the firepit and waited for his eyes to adjust to the dark.

The very moment his eyes at last adjusted to the dimness of the cave, he cautiously approached the area where the pup's clamour had emanated. Even with the daylight trickling in, it was still too dark to see anything beyond the central chamber of the wolf den. He pressed forward like a lone warrior. He had to duck, to keep his head from striking one of the jagged rock formations of the enclosing walls.

Upon reaching what felt like the rear of the cave, he was overwhelmed by a rank stench. He almost gagged at the overpowering stink. Breathing through his mouth allowed him to carry on. He heard the whimpering before he saw the pup.

The lone wolf pup tried its best to stay hidden, nestled amongst a group of six dead brethren, each one with a combination of white and ashen decomposing fur. Fleetingly, he wondered, *Had that pup survived because of the rabbit head he left by the fire last night?* and *Was that the cause of the stench connected to this carnage?*

Jackson knelt and whistled.

The pup whined anxiously and let out a small high-pitched bark. Jackson whistled again, and a growl echoed from somewhere in the darkness. He leapt to his feet and looked around wildly, his eyes darting around the cavern. The wolf pup got up and scurried into a large, sloped side-area of the cave. Jackson was hard at its heels. He rounded the corner, and there lay the pup's mother, helpless in a stinking waller of its own mess and shredded fur. The stench where she lay was strong but bearable. The pup was taking refuge behind its suffering mother.

Jackson cautiously approached the mother wolf, his rifle resting at his side. The wolf growled and strained to get to her feet but was unable to rise from her bloodied side. Her two front paws thrashed wildly. She jerked her head from side to side, baring a mouthful of sharp teeth at Jackson.

Jackson knew what he had to do to honour his clan.

It ached his heart to see a mother of his people's clan in such agony. With tear-filled eyes, he aimed his rifle at the wolf's head. She ceased thrashing and stared back up at him with pain-filled eyes.

"PA? DID YOU HEAR WHAT I SAID?" asked Jed in plain English. He tugged on the sleeve of his daydreaming father.

"Sorry, son. What's that?" said Jackson. Jed's insistence pulled him back from his reverie about the wolf clan.

"That's not a fair trade at all."

"I know, Jedediah, but we need the food, and most importantly, your younger brother needs nourishment. Mother, too. We can't continue to live on small game meat."

The trader interjected as he reappeared from the cabin's rear chambers. "Alrighty now. Here ya'll go. That's four thick strips of finely smoked moose meat. Just as you ordered."

Jackson seized the moose meat strips, placed them in a separate sack, and stuffed them into the pack. He handed the bulging pack back to Jed, and they left.

* * *

PART II

JED FOLLOWED his father out into the trading post's courtyard and shot a curious glance over his shoulder. He winced at the fur trader's hideous smile.

Beyond the courtyard, A subtle breeze whispered through the evergreen pines, sounding like the low hushed murmurs of well concealed little people. The setting sun was veiled behind a blanket of impenetrable winter clouds, its magnificence dimming in the onset of a violet evening.

"You take point with the mare. I'll ride behind on the toboggan," ordered Jackson in Anishinaabe. Jed did as he was told and hoisted himself onto the back of the bay mare. She let out a neigh and bobbed her head up and down as she always did when someone mounted her sturdy back.

Jed watched as his father stashed the pack and their gear in the toboggan's crate, tucked them in firmly, and clambered aboard the rear of the toboggan. He slung his rifle across his chest like a sentry and nodded at Jed, declaring them ready to be on the move.

Their horse and sleigh tracks from an hour ago were already concealed, replaced with a mist of icy particles gliding across the pack snow like fog. Jed knew the route well; he used distinguishable trees and other landmarks as his guides, just like his father and their fathers before had taught them.

They had been following their unseen trail for an hour through the serene midwinter evening. The setting sun presented the sprawling woodlands with a magnificent sky of lavender twilight, which seemed to radiate off the snow-packed grounds before them.

"Halt," ordered Jackson in a low yell. His voice

echoed roughly in the frosty twilight air.

Jed tugged gently on the mare's reins, and she came to a snow-crunching halt. He twisted his head around. "What is it?"

Jackson silently replied by pointing with an open hand to their immediate right, toward the direction of a large meadow obscured by ice fog.

Jed scanned the horizon until he made out a pack of slow-moving silhouettes in the distance. "What do we do?" he asked in Anishinaabe.

"We wait and see," Jackson said, clutching the rifle.

In the winter breeze, Jackson and Jed waited for the silhouettes to come closer until they could see it was three men travelling with two horses and a sleigh.

"Howdy folks," hollered one of the travellers, who rode a horse hitched to the sleigh. He was a tall man draped in a brown woollen coat and frayed buckskin trousers. His face was covered by a large shaggy beard while on his head he wore a wrinkled and tatty felt fedora.

"Hello, fellow traveller," said Jackson, sounding as much like the white travellers as he could.

Jed stared in astonishment at the size of the moose on the back of the traveller's sleigh. Covered by rawhide, its protruding antlers were the size of bulky tree logs.

The two younger men were riding together on the second horse behind the sled. The one at the reins, who seemed roughly the same age as Jed, noticed the boy's gaping stare. "Freshly killed but not a few hours ago," said the boy, with a satisfied smile.

"How true," the bearded man said.

"But where did you come across such large game? It seems these parts have been cursed with a parched spell," said Jackson.

"Directly south of us, not but three hour's ride. A whole bunch of them, I tell you. Now, we must be on our way. Goodbye," said the bearded man tipping his hat at Jed and Jackson. "Heyah!" he screamed and snapped the reins, causing the tall, feather-footed stallion to pitch forward without whinnying. The two younger riders nodded and tipped their hats in sync at Jed, following the bearded man.

Their pa, Jed thought to himself.

Jed watched his own pa, staring out at the darkening meadow, immersed in deep concentration. "I will go to that place where they came from, to find the moose, Pa," he said.

Jackson looked back at Jed, thinking back at his own first hunting excursion and how he could have been better prepared. "Then you will take the mare, the toboggan, and the rifle. I will take the rest of our things back home for your mother and brother." He dismounted from the toboggan, unslung the rifle, and rummaged through the cargo crate for other provisions. He then bade Jed farewell.

PART III

JED BACKTRACKED on the horse through the deep tracks the three successful hunters had left. Not an hour into his ride, the tracks were deteriorated by drifting snow generated by the winter wind.

Twilight was eventually replaced by the sapphire glow of the half-moon and the twinkling of the ancient grandfathers peering down from the darkened heavens.

In the low howl of the wind, the bay mare's heavy foot tramps seemed to echo through the dense air. Jed had left the meadow and was once again among a dense swath of unfamiliar woodland. He was on his own and left to use the successful methods of hunting passed down from generations of his father's bloodline.

Hopefully the three riders were right about big game in that unknown area.

"ARE YOU ABSOLUTELY SURE he is ready to be out there on his own?" Madeleine asked Jackson in Anishinaabe.

"Yes, of course he is," said Jackson. "I was twelve when I set out on my first hunting journey. Jed is thirteen; it is his time to hunt on his own." Jackson thrust the axe, cleaving the log in front of him in two. The baby, Felix, looked up with a startle.

"Okay, Jackson. I hope you're right about this," Madeleine said. She picked up baby Felix and disappeared into the wigwam.

Jackson sliced a few more fire logs and took a short rest. Sweat was beading on his forehead. He wondered about his decision to allow his elder son to go out on his own in search of moose. He was worried Jed wouldn't be able to handle a full-grown bull on his own, but he would likely be successful with a calf. So long as Jed followed the right protocol in killing the moose.

A smile crossed Jackson's face. If his son was fortunate in finding big game, they would muster up a group of men and venture out for a month's worth of food. He drank some water and continued hacking up wood for the night fire.

AFTER TRAVELLING FOR DAYS in search of game, Jed came upon a sheltered valley. The night air was as tranquil as the glittering starry night sky above. The rustling wind had died down and had been replaced by a vacant winter chill. Jed and the bay mare backtracked through her hoofprints in the deep snow, illuminated by the glow of the winter solstice half-moon, until they came upon a quiet grove that would protect them from sight.

Jed's stomach was now empty, and a sensation of weakness progressed through his body, causing him to shiver. He was miserable at not being able to find the moose and wondered how the three hunters had been lucky enough to cross their path. Dejected, he decided to dismount and hide himself behind the toboggan to calmly wait to see if the moose would come by. He hadn't expected to fall asleep, but it was the dead cold of night when he awoke with a start. He sensed activity on the snow and as his eyes focussed on the scene, he made out a group of small animals being stalked by a grey wolf. Jed spent six rounds from his bolt action rifle, three of them lucky enough to hit their intended targets. Two rabbits ... and the wolf.

DAYS HAD PASSED since his son had struck out on his own—many more than Jackson had originally predicted, so he set out on foot to find him. On the trail and in the face of a blizzard, he saw a horse trudging toward him, with what looked like a defeated warrior slouched on its back. As it came nearer, he hollered in Anishinaabe. "My son, I have found you, and you are alive."

With great effort, from atop the horse's back, Jed met his father's eye, his body wracked with sickness and pain and his brows and lashes singed with frost. "Pa ... I have damned us," he mumbled as his eyes rolled back into his head.

With great effort and over several days, Jed and Jackson made their way back to their home, sometimes on foot and sometimes on the wearying horse. Cradled now in his father's arms, Jed's delirious mind wandered back to the night of the half-moon. He tried speaking to his father, but he could only unwind the epic tale of damnation in his own mind.

I ate and ate and as I was fully satisfying my hunger, a mighty bull moose came walking towards me. I raised my rifle and since the moose was framed directly in the sight, I knew I would make the kill. I held my breath and was about to squeeze the trigger when a rumbling of hooves shook the ground all around. I tried to keep my composure, the way you told me to do, pa, but some kind of colossal animal reared up on its hind legs and exploded from the tree wall, knocking the trees dead with ear-splitting cracks like gunshots. The animal made the bull moose look like the size of a newborn puppy. It scooped up the moose with its enormous, hideous claws and flung it into the air. The moose's bones splintered as it crashed to the ground; its flesh was shredded to ribbons inside the mammoth creature's mouth. As it chewed up the moose, it raked its huge head around, sweeping the air with deformed antlers.

I sunk as low as I could and ducked behind the toboggan. I dropped my rifle to the snow. It would do nothing against the wicked creature.

Then, as horrifying as it sounds, the creature began to grow. Its greyed and flaking furless hide was stretched tightly over its bones, which poked at its skin like a starved man. This impossible beast was like an undead combination of caribou, deer, and a score of other creatures, all blended together.

Then I saw its face—the decaying skeletal head of some kind of deer, with a massive rack of disfigured antlers and wicked, crimson eyes set back deeply in blackened sockets.

I gasped, and then I screamed.

The creature's head whipped around and looked directly at me with burning red eyes, pointing at me with its malformed claws. It let out a loud ear-splitting scream, like that of a thousand anguished animals, before barrelling through the snow towards me, a plume of snow and dirt blowing in the air in its wake.

I ran away faster than I ever knew I could, when I was struck by an overpowering stench of death and decay.

I heard the creature burst through the barrier of logs behind me, and it began to yell in a hoarse voice, guttural words I didn't understand at first. As I began mystically to understand his words, I lost sensation in my legs and my knees … buckled—

These were Jed's final words he recited in his head before he fully lost consciousness in his father's arms.

JED TASTED the potent tang of blood in his dry mouth. His mother was at the foot of his bed, mixing up something in a wooden bowl. She looked up at him and smiled. She then came to his side and poured a foul-tasting liquid down his throat. Jed swallowed, forced a half-hearted smile, and fell back into unconsciousness. He woke in a cold sweat; his thinking felt vague to the point that his brain was numb. His sleep had been plagued with feverish dreams of deformed shadows lurking from within the snow-covered trees around his home.

His mother, Madeleine, sat perched in a chair of woven tree bark at the far end of the fire-warmed wigwam, sorting out a number of items on a knee-high table.

Jed pushed away at the thick buffalo robe and tried to roll out of his bedding. Madeleine dropped what she was doing and ran to his side, preventing him from straining himself. She covered him up again and spoke calmly to him in Anishinaabe, but in his muddled state, he couldn't understand what she was saying. He lay his head back down on his pillow of rabbit furs. He drank from a cup in his mother's hands, and sleep came painlessly and fast once again.

"You are very sick, my son." The voice echoed through Jed's head.

Jed slowly raised his aching head to meet his father's gaze. Jackson sat on the woven tree bark chair, taking Madeleine's place in the vigil. Strings of long dark hair were strewn across his tired face, and his chiselled jawline seemed to quiver slightly in the light of the fire. Jed had only ever seen his father's face flushed with such an expression when death was lingering.

"I—I think I'm ... s-starting to feel better." Jed forced the words out, trying his best not to sound weak. His throat felt as though a blend of copper and sand had been pressed through it.

"Rest now, my son." Jackson cupped his knees hard with a loud slapping sound and rose to his feet. He walked through the door and met his wife coming through with Felix at her side. Felix's big round eyes looked over at Jed from behind Madeleine's skirt.

"We mustn't ... he doesn't ... so sick ... the mare is

rested now ... I will go ..." Jed couldn't exactly distinguish who was saying what over their hushed whispers, but he knew his father was leaving to go somewhere. The fragmented murmurs between his parents came haltingly in waves to Jed's fevered mind. His mind drifted, and he was panicking with thirst.

After a few minutes' deliberation with Madeleine, Jackson turned and peered at his son with eyes full of worry. He nodded curtly, then departed from the wigwam, leaving Madeleine with Felix to watch over Jed.

Madeleine knelt by Jed and as if reading his fevered mind, she offered him a wooden cup. "Here you go, my boy. Drink." He took the carved wooden cup in his palms and drank without question. The cool water trickled down his throat, with an invigorating coolness like icy fingers gently stroking at a fiery surface.

"I—I will be better soon, mother," Jed said unconvincingly.

"My son, does it pain you to speak?" she asked in Anishinaabe.

Jed sipped more from the cup and averted his tired gaze to watch Felix, scrambling with his short legs to get atop the woven bark chair. Jed had not understood the words his mother had just spoken to him.

After a time, Madeleine placed her calming hand on Jed's shoulder. The beauty and serenity of her face was amplified by the tint of the swaying fire flames. Finally, she haltingly asked in English, "Did you eat something out there that caused you to become sick?"

She sat quietly, waiting for a spoken answer.

"W-W-Wolf," Jed exhaled in a choke of words.

She leaned in closer, as if she had not heard him right. "Wolf?" she asked.

He nodded fretfully.

Her eyes widened with terror confirming her worst fear that her son had consumed a brother of their People's clan. It was taboo to eat the flesh and organs of their people's clan brother. She stared at her ailing son in dismay and let out a loud gasp. As she got to her feet, she began to sob uncontrollably. She picked up Felix and staggered out of the wigwam, not wanting to alarm Jed with her anguished cries.

PART IV

JACKSON HAD BEEN TAUGHT by his father from a young age to be one of the best trackers of their section of the woodlands. With relative ease, he'd managed to discover the spot where his son had ventured off by himself. A pack of grey wolves were scrounging around the area; their noses dug deep into the snowy ground. He shot a single round in the air, causing them to run off into the woods. He searched the area for anything he could use to identify what had gotten his son so ill.

An array of messily strewn paw prints and deep tracks led him to an area surrounded by downed logs and thick, skeletal shrubs. Jackson searched the spot and came across a heap of bones gleaming in the sunlight, their whiteness nearly masking them in the snow. He knelt down, studied the bones more closely, and when he realized what he was looking at he stumbled backward, nearly falling over himself trying to get away from what he was seeing.

He regained his footing and dashed through the snow to mount the horse with the objective to rush home to his family.

* * *

THE SUN was beginning to set below the barbed treetops, but Jackson had yet to return. Madeleine and Felix were outside by the fire, seeking the safety of the outdoors for fear of what might be brewing inside the wigwam.

She heard a horse whinny, and Jackson galloped toward them, reining in hard beside the fire. "Madeleine, I know why our son has fallen ill," he said in Anishinaabe.

"Yes, I too know," she replied

Jackson drew the horse around in a circle, his eyebrows knotted in confusion.

"What is it that you have found?" Madeline asked.

"Bones," muttered Jackson. "But they w—" he was interrupted by a loud croaking cry from inside the wigwam.

"How is he?" Frightened by what he might hear, Jackson peered over Madeleine's shoulder toward the wigwam.

"He has gotten worse since you have been away. I fear that soon he will be our son no longer," she said softly.

"We must make him safe." Jackson dismounted and headed inside the wigwam. He saw that Madelaine had already swaddled Jeb in a buffalo robe but knowing what might come next, he leaned over and lashed Jed's body, chest to foot, with heavy buckskin strips. Jed's eyes were closed but his head jerked violently from side to side. "Let him sleep through this horrible lucid dream. That way, he'll not remember it when he awakens," she whispered softly.

Jackson rose and faced his wife. "We must build him his own wigwam, for it is not safe for him to stay in here and we cannot put him out to sleep in the cold."

"In the morning, my love. For now, let us attend to our ailing son and keep him calm and protected as we can."

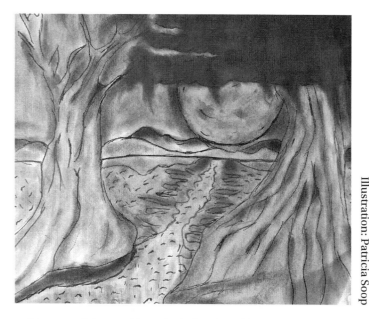

Illustration: Patricia Soop

He stepped forward into the light of the full moon, his feet crunching in the snow with a sound like snapping bones.

IN HIS DREAM, Jed was by himself. He was wearing the soft fur of a wolf, which kept him warm from the icy squall swirling about him. The winter air was heavy with the stink of death. Bare trees enveloped him on either side. He stepped forward into the light of the full moon, his feet crunching in the snow with a sound like snapping bones.

A sudden movement from the corner of his eye caught his attention. He stopped and peered into the dark, impenetrable wall of trees.

More movement.

A silhouette darker than the surrounding shadows loomed within the trees. He stared intently through the shadows and flinched at a loud raspy whisper, which seemed to reach him with the wintery wind.

"Com-i-i-ing for you-u-u," the hoarse voice hissed.

The shadow began to fade from view when an ear-splitting wail rose from within the gloom of the trees.

JACKSON WOKE in the woven bark chair. He glanced around the fire-warmed wigwam. Madeleine was

---

Evil appeared in his eyes. He spat and started screaming with a shrill voice much higher than his youthful voice should permit. He screeched in a foreign language with deep guttural undertones.

---

soundly asleep with Felix in her arms on a makeshift bed of thick buffalo robes. The fire was down to a few glowing embers. He met the gaze of his ill son.

Jed stared back at his father with a vacant look in his gleaming eyes.

"My son, are you feeling better yet?" Jackson asked.

As Jed stared at his father, evil appeared in his eyes. He spat and started screaming with a shrill voice much higher than his youthful voice should permit. He screeched in a foreign language with deep guttural undertones. He strained to get free from his bedding but was bound tightly from the chest down by the thick buffalo robe which Jackson had secured around him.

The monstrous sounds woke Madeline and Felix.

Felix began to shriek in terror, the terrifying screech a child makes when deathly afraid.

"Get Felix outside!" Jackson yelled as he leapt to his feet to retrieve something from the ground. Madeleine scooped up the wailing Felix and rushed outside.

What seemed like hours passed, the heartless sounds of a youth falling into madness rising from their home. Madeleine built a small fire outside for herself and Felix, and she began to build a new wigwam. Their home was now unusable.

Jackson at last emerged from the wigwam. His face was drenched in sweat, and his long hair hung in messy strands. "He is unconscious again. For now," he sighed. He stumbled and fell hard onto the snowy ground.

Madeleine approached his side. "Have we lost our son?" she asked as she helped him to his knees and placed a robe for him to sit on.

"I don't know." He shot Madeleine a disheartened look. "I must go to the village and gather a group of men and a medicine man. I fear I won't be strong enough once he wakes up."

JACKSON GALLOPED through the midwinter countryside toward the village as fast as the mare's muscled legs would take them. He knew he didn't have much time before Jed would awaken again, and he knew surely that his wife would not be able to handle him on her own.

Madeleine was busy constructing the new wigwam when she heard quiet sounds from the wigwam. "Mama, mama!" Her son's mournful cry pierced her with its anguish.

Madeline rushed back into the wigwam. It was

cold inside; the fire had long since gone out. There, bound tightly, was Jed. He looked at his mother and pleaded for her to help him. She crept up cautiously to free her anguished son. As she got within arm's reach, he thrashed violently, with his teeth gnashing at her gloveless, outstretched hands. He began to squirm, trying in vain to get free of his tightly wrapped restraint. His voice erupted into a hideous screaming growl, shouting at Madeleine in an inhuman guttural tongue. She stumbled backward out of the wigwam and fell to the cold blanket of snow.

She sat sobbing in the snow. Her son was gone.

WITHIN HIS DELUSION, Jed stood valiantly as the uncanny shadow re-emerged from within the thickness of the snow-covered trees. He took a few steps back, just as a tall, furry man-beast stepped out from the shadows.

"Do not fear me, for I am here to aid you," it taunted him in a strange language that Jed found he could understand clearly as his own.

"Who—who are you?" Jed asked.

"There is no time!" the beast roared. "They are coming. You must defend your family at once."

Before Jed could object, the beast stepped back into the shadows and vanished.

"They-r-r-e upon you-u-u-u," it whispered .

Jed awoke in the cold of the empty wigwam. There was no fire, only a thick buffalo robe to keep him warm. With new-found strength in his arms, he tore off the restraints with ease.

He felt like himself again. No aching muscles. No fever. No more cold and hot sweats.

He rose to his feet and stretched out his stiff limbs.

Hunger was the only thing that tormented him. His stomach growled.

As he moved silently through the wigwam, he heard movement in the snow just outside the thick woven fabric. He stopped to listen. Instantly he recognized the yaps and whines of a hungry wolfpack.

Have they found me? Jed wondered if the wolves had mustered a hunting party—and searched for him relentlessly—for killing and eating one of their own. He knew they were there to do the same to him as he had done to them.

He thought about protecting his family. A quick search of the wigwam found only a small carving knife. "It will have to do," he whispered.

He crept to the door and split a small opening to peek out.

There they were, seven in all. Six bulky adult wolves and a wolf pup all stood sniffing at the ground and his family's belongings. They stood defiantly, with dripping tongues and hunger in their yellow eyes. "If ever a wolf attacks you, go straight for the neck with a strong grip." Or, in this case, a carving knife. His pa's teaching echoed through his dulled senses.

Jed inhaled deeply and burst out through the wigwam door. The first wolf he caught by surprise. Jed sailed across the snow and sliced through the wolf's neck, a steady stream of blood darkening the snow at his feet. It fell limp to the frozen ground.

Jed continued moving fast and stealthily as the remaining wolves looked up in surprise. He rushed at the next two standing around the fire. He kicked hard at the first, sending it crashing and shrieking into the flames.

Before the other wolf had a chance to react, Jed was upon it, thrusting the little knife deep into the side of its neck, just below its pointed ears. The knife pierced through its neck bone, and the wolf let out a loud, gurgling howl before falling dead to the ground.

Jed looked up with hate burning in his eyes. The remaining adult wolves scampered off with their bushy tails tucked tightly between their legs.

In the pack's hasty retreat, they had forgotten their youngling.

Jed stared at the helpless young pup. He didn't want to have to kill such a young wolf, but then ..."Kill or be killed!" The guttural whisper of the man-beast cut through the stagnant winter breeze.

Without thinking, Jed stormed the terrified wolf pup and slashed the knife across his neck. He watched the pup's head slip away from its body and tumble across the blood-splattered snow. The pup's dead blue eyes stared sightlessly up at Jed.

Hands covered in blood, Jed scanned the camp for any remaining wolves. The surviving wolves had scurried off; he suspected they wouldn't be back.

He smiled.

Now to find his family.

A SMALL BOY and his big sister wrestled playfully near the village in a small clearing when a group of three men emerged on horseback from out of the bush. They looked exhausted.

"They have returned!" someone yelled.

An assembly of men and women rushed to the small party.

The two boys ceased their game and watched as some of their family attended to the three men.

The boy and his sister snuck up to the group, making sure to stay hidden behind a big tree. She overheard one of the men speak in Anishinaabe:

"We must gather a large group of our best hunters. The Wendigo has fully grasped hold of a boy," the man said with his head bowed low. "Before they could escape, he killed his own father, mother, brother, and our medicine man."

Illustration: Patricia Soop

MAN OF GOD

THE MAN stirred peacefully awake, his eyes opening as though he'd slept right through a marvellous dream until the very ending—an ending to a dream he already couldn't remember. He analyzed the blue ceiling of the chamber in which he rested. A mesh of spiderless cobwebs and a white, chalky substance smeared the four corners of the otherwise pristine walls, the aroma of fresh paint still evident.

Flurries of emptiness brazed through his head. Empty thoughts of his current whereabouts and of yesterday's happenings. He only remembered his age and his name. Barely. "My name is Norbert ... Stricterland, and I am sixty-fi—no, sixty-six years old. And why the heck did I just say that out loud?" he said in a joyless giggle to the hollow emptiness of the room.

He heaved his legs from the burrows of smooth sheets and planted his feet on the even smoother floor. The delicate flooring radiated with a tinge of warmth like sauna-room decking. Sky-blue paint covered the entire room, ceiling and all.

"Where the heck am I?" he cautiously asked.

Norbert was used to waking up to minor aches and pains, but not this morning. He felt great like a full thirty years was knocked off his age of sixty-six.

He rubbed at his foggy eyes and took a closer examination of the room. It was small, about the size of an oversized wardrobe closet belonging to the wealthy. The bed he had just risen from was more of a cot but a comfortable one.

Norbert broke out into a jog .... The mirrored door loomed closer, looking as though it was gravitating towards him through the corridor.

A small, circular porthole of a window was recessed into the wall at the head of the bed, but all he was able to see through it was a white brightness, like two rising suns shining simultaneously. An oversized wooden desk sat in the far corner of the room, with an elaborate chair to match.

Norbert stepped cautiously toward the desk. A large, ancient-looking book rested at the corner of the rectangular desktop, bound in what seemed to be aged leather. His hands just skimmed the coating of the book's cover when a slight shock coursed through him, and a loud buzz broke the room's stillness. A narrow door with no visible framework appeared on the wall.

Curiously, Norbert took small, furtive steps towards the open door and felt along the edges with wary fingers. Nothing but pure smoothness like that of flawless sword steel slid against his fingertips.

A small voice in the core of his mind told him to step out through the narrow passageway. So he did.

The broad hallway settled outside the little room was painted in the same sky-blue fashion as the bed-chamber, with no visible cracks or crevices indicating where the floor joined the walls. The surface of the floor shone and glittered like it was fabricated out of diamond dust, while a light, refreshing mist wafted through the unblemished air.

He looked around, not knowing which way to go. Both directions seemed to fade endlessly into the vague mist. A lone man dressed in baby-blue coveralls was down the hall, scrubbing hard at the floor on his hands and knees. Beyond him, the hall stretched on for miles, narrowing like a length of square tube gradually twisting shut.

"Hello there, I think I am lost," Norbert said to the man.

The cleaner continued scrubbing at the already spotless floor without even looking up or acknowledging Norbert's presence.

"Okay, then. Suit yourself," Norbert said under his breath. He spun to face the opposite stretch of corridor, squinting at what looked to be a mirrored door at the very end.

With utmost curiosity, Norbert broke out into a jog, bounding down the hall, his bare feet slapping on the warm, spotless floor. The mirrored door loomed closer, looking as though it was gravitating towards him through the corridor.

The door slid open rapidly and soundlessly just as Norbert came within arm's reach. He slowed to a snail's pace and stepped cautiously across the threshold, feeling the warmth turn cooler.

Behind the sliding door was a windowless room, empty except for an oblong desk scattered with papers, a leather office chair turned away from the door, and a cork board on the wall adorned in photographs. A small rickety chair—meant for himself he assumed—rested on the opposite side of the sprawling desk. Not a hundred percent sure of what move he should make next, Norbert remained standing.

Abruptly, the office chair swiveled around, and a lanky man materialized, wearing thick-framed sunglasses and an old-timey, pinstripe zoot suit. "Oh, hello there, Mr. Stick...Shrincter? Aww, jeez, I'm sorry, but you're going to have to help me out here, fella. Your surname is a real tongue twister, I'm afraid," said the lanky man, his accent pitched in the east-coast, Boston style.

"It's Stricterland. And hello to you as well." Norbert then asked, "I assume you're the man who would be able to help me out?"

The mystery man leaned forward and began thumbing through a stack of papers before finally focussing his full attention on Norbert. "You are correct, Mr. Stricterland. Did I say it right? Good. And yes, that's what I am here for." He motioned to the only vacant chair. "Please, have yourself a seat."

Norbert repositioned the chair and sat down. He didn't bother composing himself. "So, you know who I am, then?" he asked, although he figured he already knew the answer.

The mystery man lowered his face and stared up at Norbert over the tops of his tinted glasses. "Mmhmm. Again, correct. Now, this will be your one and only chance to ask me any questions. Go."

"Well, first of all, who are you?"

The man looked insulted. "Come on now, is that

really a question you're curious about? I mean obviously, you must be wondering about this here place." The man flailed his open hands abruptly in the air, causing a breeze past Norbert's face.

Norbert nodded reluctantly.

"Fine," he snapped. "My name is Vinnie—Vincenzo. But that's all I am gonna tell ya. Now if you will, please, throw me a more suitable question."

"Where am I? Am I dead?" asked Norbert.

Vinnie removed his sunglasses and slammed his face into his palm, exhaling deeply. "That's two questions," he said impatiently. "That's two whole answers I gotta explain. How about the latter, first?"

"Okay, then. Fine, the latter."

"In here, we don't call it dead, see. There's no such word for it since your soul can't truly die, now, can it?"

"So, what you're saying is ... that this is the afterlife?"

"Bingo!" shouted Vinnie, pointing a two-finger gun gesture at Norbert's chest. "We have ourselves a winner, ladies and gentlemen." He finished hollering rowdily, and quieted, his mood turning drab before saying: "And as for where you currently are?" He smiled slightly, his eyes burrowing into Norbert's. "Where do ya think you are?"

"Heaven?" Norbert answered conceitedly.

Vinnie looked uneasily away from Norbert and began rifling through his stack of papers. "You ain't in Heaven, pal. I'll tell you what ..." he said, murmuring more to himself.

"Wait, what? Why am I not in Heaven?" Norbert demanded.

"Ugh, this is the part of my job I hate the most—having to explain why people like you are not in Heaven. Did you even have a gander at the handbook in your cell? It's all in there in plain ol' English. Everything."

Norbert was taken aback like an invisible knife of frost had sliced through him, his mouth dropping open and his eyebrows elevating up his forehead. "Did you just say 'cell'? And that huge, endless textbook in there was a handbook?"

"Correcto," Vinnie replied nonchalantly, leaning back in his chair and interlocking his fingers behind his head, his slight grin reforming.

"But I am a preacher of the Good Word, a—a Man of God, for Heaven's sake. I devoted my entire life to the Almighty."

"Yes, that too is correct. And please, take it easy on the blasphemy around here," Vinnie huffed, his eyes darting to the papers strewn on his desk. He combed his fingers through his greasy slicked-back, pompadour hair. "But you didn't really think that some of your ... actions, let's call them, would have gone unnoticed by Him? Like ya said, you are a man of God, so you clearly knew that He would be watching you at all times. And not to mention, what you did is just plain sinful."

"That is preposterous," screamed Norbert, ejecting himself from the rickety chair. "How dare you accuse me of such—such hideous crimes.?"

"Ugh, again with this dang job," snapped Vinnie, "and please sit down." He leaned forward to wag an accusing finger at Norbert. "You people think that just because you got away with your crimes in the past life, you don't have to pay for them in the afterlife? Well, guess what. That ain't the case here. Don't believe me? Here, have a gander for yourself." He skated a small heap of stapled papers across the desktop toward Norbert.

Norbert curiously flicked through the stack of papers, skimming over reports of the numerous wrongdoings he had accumulated throughout his years of employment at Mountview Residential School, and later a reform school for boys. "So what, then, am I in Hell?" he asked, dropping his gaze to the floor.

"Nope, sorry there, Father. I'm happy to inform you there is no such place—or at least for regular ol' folk like yourself. You don't actually believe the Almighty would condemn his own creations, his children, so to speak, to an eternity of burning? Hah! And at the hands of some scraggly looking fella with horns, dressed in a red suit, poking at ya with a three-pronged spear?"

Norbert heaved a heavy sigh, rubbing his fingers through what was left of his balding scalp. "Okay, then. Where am I?"

"A man of God as yourself should know that each and every soul that passes on must atone for their past life of sins. There's just no way around it, see."

"So, this is purgatory. Is this place some kind of a prison?"

"Very correct. Now you're rolling on the ball."

"Well ... how long can I expect to be here?"

Vinnie quickly answered, "Put it this way. How long did ya live consequence free from the first time you sexually assaulted that helpless boy—what was his name?" He skimmed over a top sheet. "Yes, here we are. George Leonard Williams, also known as Piita in his ancestral language. And that instance is just one of twenty-two boys ... and girls."

Norbert felt a hot surge of blood flush in his face "You must think I'm such a monster," he whispered.

"I've met worse. Trust me," Vinnie retorted unemotionally, picking up a pen and fiddling with it. "But unfortunately, in your case, your direct actions did set in motion a chain of events; meaning that your victims, unable to overlook their childhood and adolescent years of pain, succumbed to becoming drug addicts, alcoholics, criminals ... the list goes on.

You see, these individuals were unable to live peaceful and fulfilled lives due to the unspeakable acts you forced upon them. Some of them, in turn, also have victims and will also have to, one day, reside here, where I will eventually speak to them myself—in that exact chair. Remember, though, it's not my place to make the big decisions—or any for that matter. That's up to ... well, you know who. I'm just here to answer a few questions, and then getcha settled in, see."

"I am looking at a twenty-two-year stay?" he asked.

"Nice try. We're going with eighty-eight—His ruling. I hate to be the one to inform ya. And that's Him being nice. But you're still gonna have to be re-examined once those years are up. You know? To see if you're qualified to live upstairs with the regulars." Vincent said, staring up at the ceiling of blue and white.

"What? Well, is there any chance of early parole?" Norbert asked in utter disbelief, hoping for an easy answer to lighten up the sombre atmosphere.

Vinnie stared at him with unfaltering eyes. "Again, sorry to inform ya, there is no parole here, and no recompenses for good behaviour. Nothing but time for you to do penance for your unpunished life of sin. Now, are there any more questions you'd like answered?"

"What if I lose my mind, confined to solitary detention for so long?"

"The good news is that crazy don't exist here, along with obligatory, living body bathroom breaks." Vinnie eyed the ceiling again, the view portraying a shifting cloud of vivid whiteness. "He made sure of that. You still get fed, you still sleep, you still ... well. You get the picture. He wanted to keep some mortality traits alive here."

After a moment of silent contemplation, Norbert asked, "Will I ever meet Him?"

Vinnie burst out laughing, a nasal laugh that ended in a coughing fit. "Not ever while you're locked up, tell ya that much. Now, is that it? Any more questions?"

Head bowed in shame, Norbert rose slowly out of his chair, shoulders slumped and with a heavy head. "No. I'm sure the rest will be answered for me in the handbook."

"Yeah, well, that's what it's there for, see. Now, I have a lot on my plate." Vinnie rose from his chair and waved Norbert toward the door without offering a handshake. "The guy outside will guide ya back to your cell."

Norbert slowly staggered toward the mirrored door, dragging his feet. He stopped just short of the closed door and turned to face Vincent. "Wait, just one more question?"

Vinnie exhaled loudly. "Okay then. Shoot."

"Who are you, and why are you here, doing this job?"

"Long story short," Vinnie answered. "I was once a cold-blooded gangster. You may have heard of me—you may not have. I've been here eighty years, and I will continue to be here a heckuva lot longer. And don't ya think for one second that I like this job. I haven't seen the outside of this room in thirty long years. That's all I'm gonna tell ya. Now go." He sat back down and swung around in his office chair, again facing the corkboard adorned with photographs.

The mirrored door opened with a slight hiss. Norbert whirled around, stepped through, and was immediately met by the custodian in the blue suit who had been mopping the floor.

"I'll take you back to your cell now," said the man with a smile.

Norbert glanced from the floor to the man's face, which he now studied more closely. This was an Indigenous man who looked much like the many youths, and young men and women, who had come and gone through the doors of Mountview Residential School.

The two men walked in silence through the impossibly long, doorless corridor, until they finally came to the

---

"I'm sorry," he said softly, tears

trickling down his anguished face.

"I'm so sorry for what I've done to your people.

Please—oh please, will you forgive me?

---

only opening along the wall of ceaseless blue.

"Here we are. And hey, don't worry," the custodian said, still smiling politely, "it's not actually like what Vincenzo said. You can get rewards for good behaviour. Just look at me, I get to leave my own cell and roam these halls."

Norbert stood quietly and wondered what the Indigenous man had done to get himself into this place of residence. He took a sluggish step forward and then stopped, his body midway through the threshold, before turning toward the custodian. "I'm sorry," he said softly, tears trickling down his anguished face. "I'm so sorry for what I've done to your people. Please—oh please, will you forgive me?"

The custodian regarded Norbert kindly. "You know what? On behalf of my people, I will accept your apology today. Now, please, try and get yourself some rest. You have nothing but time from here on out." With that said, he winked at Norbert, turned, and walked back up the hall into the hazy mist of blue.

Norbert stepped inside his cell.

He inched a few paces and whirled his body around to see that the door was no longer there, replaced by the vivid wall of blue. He returned to his cot and sat down, staring at his bare feet on the shiny floor.

As he looked up, his eyes were immediately struck by a new arrangement of photographs affixed to a corkboard above his desk, much as he had seen hanging behind Vinnie. How had he not noticed these before?

He leaned in for a better look.

The scenes depicted in the many pictures were familiar, but some weren't. They were all taken in a style of candid voyeurism and from a high angle—views only made possible by someone hiding and unseen. A view from God.

There was one thing the snapshots all had in common: they were horrific.

Norbert looked away in disgust as he laid eyes on one snapshot in particular. It was a young man—a very familiar young man—standing tall and aggressive above a bruised and battered woman screaming in agony, shielding her beautiful face with her arms.

He had seen enough.

Norbert looked away, craning his head to take a better look through the small, circular porthole window at the head of the bed where he had once seen the blinding light of a double sun. The light was now gone, swapped with a picturesque view of a towering green mountain adorned in palm trees, standing tall before a magnificent white sandy beach.

Eighty-eight years is a long time, he thought as he stared in awe at the Heavenly sight. But it beats an eternity of burning in a place that doesn't even exist.

"Or does it exist?" Norbert contemplated to himself. "Perhaps it's just reserved for the living realm's most wicked of the wicked. The Christopher Columbus and Adolf Hitlers of the living world."

Whatever the correct answer was, he now had nothing but time to ponder it.

Deciding to make himself at home, he sprawled out on his cot, eyed the big brown handbook, now somehow resting on the foot of his bed, and shut his eyes. At least his cell had a blissful view, and he was still permitted to sleep in this afterlife.

For the next eighty-eight years, this place would be his home.

FOUR

A LIVELY OLD
MERRIMENT

PART I

THIS IS A PERSONAL STORY that I must tell. Or to, at least, put into words for someone else to read one day. Plain and simple. It is a most startling account of my first experiences while field researching my Indigenous blood lineage.

It began with a trip I put together in hopes of further understanding my ancestral roots. Canada was my only intended destination: Alberta and British Columbia, but last-minute plans had me incorporate Alaska into this overseas expedition. My reading and studies on the Na-Dene Peoples of the Pacific Northwest intrigued me about the State of Alaska. I supposed I would start there, then make my way southeastward through the Rocky Mountains until I arrived at the plains region of my lineage—the Blackfoot, or, as I had discovered in researching the Blackfoot tongue, Niitsitapi.

Even though I was born and raised in the great and noble country of England, I have Blackfoot blood coursing through my veins. My great-grandfather was a brave man of the Blood Tribe, hailing from an area called Bullhorn. Like many of his mates, my great-grandfather decided he would find excitement and adventure in the Great War, off in faraway lands. Exciting undertakings that reserve life couldn't provide were awaiting them if they enlisted in the Canadian Expeditionary Force, fighting boldly in the trenches of the Western Front. So, he and others from the Blood Tribe willingly enlisted.

I ferried from Alaska to British Columbia and hitchhiked my way to the small city of Prince Rupert where I stayed the night in a modest hotel.

Before ultimately being sent to the front lines, my great-grandfather spent a wee bit of time posted in England; where the CEF was based, along with The British Armed Forces. In a small Manchester pub, great-grandfather met the woman who would become my great-grandmother. The rest, as they say, is history.

I worked like a dog to be allotted the time off I required for my journey to Canada. I asked for two months off without pay, and my boss gladly permitted it, seeing all the work I had done in a year without having taken any time off.

My initial stop and the first leg of my journey began in Juneau, Alaska. I found it disheartening that I didn't happen upon any local Indigenous Peoples. I became a regular at some of the local hot-spot pubs for the three days I spent there. I then came across a brown-skinned fellow who I was sure was an Alaskan First Nation person. No luck there with the lad. He was of Mexican descent and had moved north from Houston, Texas not some two years prior. Damn, so close, I thought. But not close enough.

Prior to my trip and with careful planning, I also spent time studying the exploits of one Chris McCandless. You may recognize him easily enough as the man from the movie and book, "Into the Wild." His last stop was ultimately the unforgiving wilderness of Alaska, where he eventually lost his life due to starvation and the region's climate extremities. I gravely didn't want to end up like that poor chap, so that is why I decided to make my journey during the summer months of July and August.

From Juneau, I made my way south, island hopping across the Alexander Archipelago. I was quite blissful, to say the least, when I finally came across some of the local Tlingit People scattered amongst the islands. They found my accent and dialect quite splendid, even though it is from the working-class midlands of England. Their manner of speech was interesting too and unlike any other Caucasian Americans I had come across thus far. I decided to stay a week when I found a Tlingit family willing to take me under their wing, inviting me to live in their dwellings. I was given a brief lesson about their traditional ways of life. Just like us Brits, they too loved their seafood. I had a bloody good and unforgettable time. Along with my timely departure came the gift of a magnificently fabricated Chilcott blanket, a gift that would come in most handy in the days to follow. I was sad to leave my Tlingit hosts.

Next up was Canada, which was easy enough to access because the Canada/US border line carved right through the cluster of islands connecting Juneau to the continental mainland. I ferried from Alaska to British Columbia and hitchhiked my way to the small city of Prince Rupert where I stayed the night in a modest hotel to gather myself and plan out the rest of my southeast journey down through the mountainous woodlands of British Columbia.

While enjoying a pint by myself in the hotel lounge, a beautiful red-haired woman approached me. Her flowing scarlet hair told me she was of English ancestry herself. She had me enticed.

"Not from around here, are you?" she asked.

"How did you figure?" I replied.

She pointed to my tall glass of murky stout. "No one from around here ever orders Guinness," she snickered. "That and the fact that you're wearing hiking boots. Locals don't wear hiking boots."

"You've got me there," I said, extending my hand in greeting. "Pleasure to meet you. I'm Paxton."

She hesitated for a moment and studied me like a fretted fox. At last, she let her guard down and took my rugged hand in her silky palms. "It's nice to meet you too. My name is Heidi. Are you from London?" she asked.

"Oooh, sorry Miss Heidi, I'm afraid you're quite off by a longshot."

"Okay, okay, no I got this, I'm good with this kind of stuff," she blurted. "Let's see, you're from.... I'm going to say... Manchester."

"Ahh, now I'm impressed. Will you join me?" I pulled a stool out for her from under the bar. "Let me buy you a drink. Please, it's the least I can do."

She plopped down on the stool beside me. "I'll take a Kokanee" she politely demanded of the bartender.

"So, what brings you here?" asked Heidi with a smile.

"Vacation, you could say," I said.

"Welcome to the club. Or at least once upon a time."

"I beg your pardon?"

"Oh, my bad. I'm actually from the States—Arizona, to be exact. I hate the dry heat, so I came here for a visit, came back again, and just sorta never left."

"Ahh, that sounds most splendid."

"Yes, it does, doesn't it?" she said playfully.

I had made my first lady friend (excluding my Tlingit host's wife), and then from there, we got ourselves piss drunk like two college students on vacation. I had my first-ever Kokanee, and I could say it was a delight. Then I had more—

PART II

I WOKE UP the next day on my unforgiving hotel bed with an eradicator of a headache. It felt as though the whole of London Bridge had fallen down right on top of my noggin. My first Canadian hangover. I glanced around. There were absolutely no signs that I had entertained a guest for the night. I shrugged off the notion that I'd brought the woman from the bar back to my room and decided I should carry on with my original travel plans. I washed up, rehydrated and proceeded with my hitch-hiking excursion.

I used to spend whatever vacation time I could muster hiking, climbing, and camping out in the Swiss Alps, but the BC landscape was much wilder. As an avid outdoorsman though, I was excited rather than intimidated. My time in the Alps would play a major role in my trek between Prince Rupert and, ultimately, Calgary, Alberta. The crisp mountain air was like inhaling the breath of the Almighty. Nothing at all like the air in midland cities.

While trekking down the side of the highway, I heard the sound of hissing brakes and blow-off pressure valves of an enormous semi-truck from behind me. The massive truck nearly jackknifed to a stop right in my path, making me dive into the deep, grassy ditch. I heard an offer and climbed aboard.

With his shaggy beard, beer-keg belly and hard-pressed teeth, the truck driver's appearance was quite scruffy, to say the least. But he turned out to be quite a charming lad. He introduced himself as Michael and despite looking ten years older, he told me he was twenty-eight.

Another thing he said was that the highway we travelled on was known as the Highway of Tears, a foreboding title if ever there was one. He explained the Highway of Tears derived its name from the numerous women, mostly Indigenous, who had gone missing or who had been murdered on that lonely, desolate stretch of backwoods road.

It was coming on night, the sun slowly sinking beyond the westerly peaks of the towering mountains, the last tints of yellow and gold lingering above the mountain crests like heaven's halos. I peered outside my window at the infinite array of rapidly passing evergreen trees, their shades of green growing darker and darker with every fading shift into the distance.

That was when Michael brought it upon himself to start telling me some eerie tales about that remote highway. He certainly had a knack for telling his ghost stories to roadside ramblers like me. One such story made my arms break out into gooseflesh. He lowered his voice and increased it at times for dramatic effect, just like the professional narrators from audiobook recordings.

One story he told was about a young hitchhiking tourist, like myself, who was left all alone on the side of the deserted highway. It was getting late, and therefore the fellow had no other choice but to set up camp for the night. He decided to set up not too far from the highway, but he also didn't want to be too close in case a semi was to have an accident and roll off the road. Closer to the road meant he might flag down an approaching vehicle if the chance arose.

He was busy putting up his tent when he glanced up just in time to see a woman stumbling from the dense scrubland's remote darkness, and it looked like she was in trouble. He dropped what he was doing and hurried towards the woman to see if she was okay. About thirty feet away from her, he stopped dead in his tracks. Even from that distance and through fog that was rolling in through the fading light, he could see she looked like death. Where her eyes should have been were only empty sockets as black as char.

Her ashen skin glowed a desiccated tint of green and he could see blackened blood vessels protruding on her forearms. Her dark red, oozing mouth was open, but no sound escaped. Fear overpowered him and he bolted back to the lonely highway where he trekked down the meridian for hours in the dark until a willing motorist picked him up. He never dared to go back to the site to retrieve his abandoned gear.

"That's got to be an old wives' tale, or whatever you people call them around here," I said to Michael, all the while praying that we didn't break down in the middle of that highway's foggy blackness.

"I shit'cha not. Happened to a friend of a friend of mine. A friend of a friend who just happened to be the willing motorist who picked up that guy." Michael slowly swivelled his face toward me, a look of firm steadfastness draped over his expression.

"So, your friend's friend picked up this traveller, then?" I asked.

"Yep, hell, I believe it, what with all the women who've been killed in ruthless ways on this road. Ya know what some people say—if someone is killed in an unnatural way, then their spirit is cursed to roam the land until they find their peace.

"Speak of the devil," Michael said, turning up the stereo. AC/DC's Highway to Hell blasted from the speakers.

"Charming," I muttered under my breath.

The remaining stretch of the late-night road journey was filled with the brash sounds of headbanger rock. Before I knew it, I drifted off to sleep.

I awoke alone in the dead silence of the semi truck's cabin. The still air hummed with the scent of fake fresh pine from the air freshener dangling from the passenger visor. I raked my head around in search of Michael. The enormous parking lot was dimly lit, with the black pavement radiating a wet glow.

The silence was suddenly broken by the loud squealing of the driver side door as it wrenched open. "Well shit the bed, sleeping beauty's awake. Ya hungry?" Michael asked.

"Where are we?" I asked, half out of my wits.

"Houston. But not the Texas kind. We're about halfway to Prince George."

"How long until Prince George, then?"

"Still a ways. Here, you look hungry." He tossed me a warm, aluminum-wrapped package. "Grilled cheese and fries, on me."

"I can pay you b—"

"No, no. This one's on me, my friend. I'm just

relieved to have had some company. Trust me when I say, it gets lonely—and way too scary—on that desolate highway."

"Well thank you, mate. I certainly appreciate it," I said and chowed down the truck-stop food faster than I'd like to admit.

"You're very welcome," Michael said, smiling.

That night, we chipped in on an old roadside motel and carried on with our road trip as soon as we awoke.

The remaining trip was alive with more of his tales and adventures, and he didn't leave out any of his camp-fire ghost stories. None of the rest of them left me with the same sense of dread as that first one had, though. My first taste of a Canadian ghost story was seared into my mind.

PART III

MICHAEL AND I parted ways in Prince George. We swapped phone numbers and I gave him a firm hand-shake before I clambered out of his big rig. Once again, I was on my own to carry on with my expedition.

It was the dead of night. The motel lobby I stumbled into was small, with a scent of disinfectant and cigarette smoke staining the air. A small, cracked leather sofa was perched in the far corner of the room with an old beat-up wooden bench operating as a makeshift coffee table. At the forward of the small square waiting room was an even older, even-more-beat-up television that blared away an old action movie.

"What can I do for ya?" asked the motel clerk who I'm sure had been dead asleep two minutes previously.

"I'd like a room for the night, please," I said.

"Late ain't it?" said the clerk.

I gazed down at his name tag. It read: Benson.

"Mr. Benson," I said with a forced smile. "It's late alright and believe me, I deserve a good night's sleep." I grabbed my key and mounted the stairs to my room.

The shabby motel room was barely serviceable, reeking, as it did, of cigarette smoke and spilled alcohol. The faded, checkered carpet perfectly matched the worn-out blanket on the bed. I was in no position to complain though, so I climbed into bed and closed my eyes.

I stopped and hopelessly listened as my friend's screams gradually faded into the infinite darkness of the night. In this nightmare terror, I was completely alone.

Michael's tales were still on my mind. I dreamt I was back with Michael on foot in the secluded BC wilderness. We were surrounded by an impenetrable enclosure of trees, trees, and more trees, their skeletal figures seeming to creep in on us. Daylight barely pierced the tree canopy, giving the ground all around the appearance of a ceaseless evening. Fear immediately arose and pulsated through my nerves.

"We should camp soon, shouldn't we?" I asked Michael in my dream that felt so real. His face was concealed by rolling fog and shadows surrounding us. He didn't answer but kept on walking.A few minutes later, the hair on my neck stood on end. It felt like we were being watched. But all I could see was the wall of darkness and eternally shadowed tree trunks.

"Let's set up camp on that high ground, over there," I pointed at a grassy hill.

"You're the boss," Michael said.

We trekked further upwards until the bushy terrain finally began to clear and the ground flattened out. We set up camp by a large tree trunk. Michael then emptied out his backpack but all he had inside was a glimmering bottle of an unknown liquid. We drank.

After a few shots of the vile-tasting spirit, my vision began to wobble and blur like I was drugged by an anesthetic of some type.

"Are you doing okay there buddy?" asked Michael with a snicker. I looked up at his campfire-illuminated face. It quivered in shades of reds and oranges, giving it a sadistic look.

"I—I—I don't know, mate. I think it's better that I—"

Michael's ear-splitting shriek cut me short as he was ripped from where he sat and was dragged off into the darkness. I leapt to my feet and ran after the sounds of his twig snapping, dragging body, and shrill cries for help. I kept up with the sounds of Michael's cries until the campfire faded from sight and I was surrounded by nothing but cold and empty blackness. I stopped and hopelessly listened as my friend's screams gradually faded into the infinite darkness of the night. In this nightmare terror, I was completely alone in a forest of shadow that I knew harboured an unseen enemy.

I awoke in a dead panic and rolled off my bed onto the floor, my arms and feet twisted up in the loose bed sheets. My mind still resonated with Michael's dying cries for help. Stumbling in the moonlit darkness of the motel room, I searched around in my clothes and grabbed my cellphone, At last, finding it, I punched in Michael's number, not caring what hour it was. It felt at that moment like it was life or death.

"Hello. Mike here," said the groggy voice, the sounds of his heavy motor rumbling in the background.

"Michael. It's Paxton. Sorry about the late call, but I just had a terrible dream about you. I needed to know if you were doing alright."

"Let me guess...was it that damned Highway of Tears?" he asked, his voice portraying no such fear such as mine.

"Yes, you're right. How did you ever—"

Michael burst out in a laugh. "I knew my stories would get ya."

I was relieved that it was just my overactive imagination. "Alright mate. Good to know you're okay, then. Look, I better get back to sleep, and let you get back to the road. I'll be in touch."

"Alright my friend. Don't dream so damn hard next time," Michael said before hanging up.

I returned to my musty-smelling bed, closed my eyes, and resumed my trip to the land of sleep. No more dreams of that dreaded highway returned.

PART IV

THE NEXT DAY, I had no problem at all finding rides—I didn't even have to stick out my thumb. People like Good Samaritan Joseph noticed my big pack and decided to take a chance. I rode with him for over an hour before he slowed his speed near an offramp.

"Well, my exit is comin' up. I recommend you stay put and have yourself a gander at Barkerville. It's a remarkable little town," said Joseph.

"Why thank you, mate. I appreciate the gesture, but perhaps it's best that I keep on heading east before it gets too late."

"I hear you on that one." Joseph exited the turnpike and slowly pulled over to the shoulder of the highway. "Good luck, eh," he said and extended his arm in a good-mannered gesture.

"Thank you, Joseph. Cheers and best wishes," I said as I shook his hand in appreciation. And just like that, another good-hearted Canadian was out of my life.

Following the last of a number of rides I thumbed through BC and into Alberta, I waited alongside Highway 1 as a few cars sped past me before darting across the road. Keeping a good pace, I trekked down the grassy ditch of the highway, ultimately settling beneath an overpass to study my map and escape the dust of the road and the searing summer heat. I was doing my calculations on the length of time it would take to walk the rest of the way to Calgary when a truck pulled over.

"Hey there, stranger. You need a lift?" yelled a man through his passenger window.

I looked up in surprise, astounded at how kind and trusting these Canadians were to me. "Yeah," I yelled back, "I could most definitely use a lift." I climbed to my feet, jogged over to the truck, unshouldered my pack, and tossed it in the cargo box. As I hopped in I noticed a "Pow-Wow Fever" sticker on the glove compartment but it didn't carry any meaning for me at first glance.

"How do you do," I said, offering my hand in gratitude. "I'm Paxton."

"Holeh, an Englishman." He gripped my hand tightly. "I'm Tyson. Buckle up and let's get a-rollin."

"Righty ho," I said and then mimicked him

good-naturedly, "Let's get a-rollin'"

"So, where y'off to, there, brother?" Tyson asked as he put the truck in gear and peeled off the gravel shoulder. He spoke with a slight accent, similar to the Tlingit people I had stayed with.

"Well, I'd like to get to Calgary, if you're heading that way?"

"Yes sir, I sure am—and then some."

"Beg your pardon, mate?"

"I'm just by-passing Calgary. I'm actually heading down south."

"South. You wouldn't happen to be going near the Blood Tribe or around there, would you?" I asked eagerly.

"No shit? That's exactly where I'm headed. That's where I am from," he said with a chuckle.

I was overcome with delight. His accent and the Pow-Wow sticker now made total sense to me. He must be an Indigenous man. "Well, I'll be ... it truly is a small world after all."

"Sorry?" asked Tyson.

"Hmm, where to start." I pondered for a moment, trying not to betray my excitement. "I'll just come and say it. I am headed to the Blood Tribe too. You see, my great-grandfather hailed from there."

Tyson shot me a sideward glance. "Well holy shit on a stick. Bet you're glad I came along then, eh?"

"Very. Where are you coming from, if you don't mind my asking?"

"Wedding up in Banff—my sister's wedding. I was in the lineup, and now just making my way home. Boy I'll tell you what though, I'm sure as hell feeling the effects from last night."

"Was it a traditional wedding?" I inquired.

"I dunno what your concept of a traditional wedding is. But yeah, you can say that there was some tradition. We had a drum group sing, and an Elder bless the ceremony. The booze part wasn't quite as much tradition, though."

"Did the groom wear a headdress or something?"

Tyson burst out laughing so hard he nearly lost his grip on the steering wheel. Once he'd regained his composure, he asked, "Where did you say you were from, again?"

"I didn't. I hail from the city of Manchester, born and raised... Northern part of England."

"Well, that figures. I'll tell you something right quick, though," Tyson said. He eyed me and waited for me to acknowledge him. "Well, first of all, not any regular Joe Schmoe Indian is allowed to sport a headdress. It must be gifted to them, or they would have to earn it. And not to mention, my sister married a napikwaan, so yeah, there you go."

"Sorry. A napee—"

"Napikwaan," snickered Tyson, "it means 'white man' in Blackfoot."

"Ahh. My first Blackfoot language lesson."

"So, your great-grandfather? Let me guess. One of the few wars that Canada has been involved in?"

"That's right," I said, "World War One." I stopped and waited for instructions for me to enlighten him further. While waiting, I briefly examined Tyson. He didn't look at all like the warriors from the pictures I had studied in school. He was brawny, like he was a regular gym-goer. His chiselled jawline complimented his dark-brown hair, which was cut short, and pomaded into a faded Caesar cut. Although he was light-skinned, there was still some natural tan to him.

He nodded at me as if to say: carry on. And I did.

"My great-grandfather came from a place called Bullhorn—" I began.

"Gee, it just keeps getting better and better, don't it! That's the section of the rez where I'm from." He tittered like a schoolboy. "Sorry, go on."

I related the story of how my Blackfoot forefather had yearned for adventure and had enlisted in the Canadian Armed Forces with his brothers and fellowship. And then how it came to be that he met my great-grandmother. It didn't end there. Tyson was very interested to know how I grew up. The differences between my coming of age and his rez upbringing, his own words, were substantial.

The remaining leg of our flat, prairie land journey was filled with stories of myself and of Tyson's. We started from our toddler years chatting about differences between rez life, and Manchester life and ended by comparing Blackfoot women with English women. From Tyson's description, I longed to meet a beautiful, caramel-skinned Blackfoot woman with flowing, jet-black hair, and narrowed eyes that pierced the soul.

"Wow. The Rocky Mountains look even more so beautiful when we're this far from them," I said, staring at the bedazzling sight of where the crimped, grey mountain slopes mingled into the indigo skyline.

"Yeah, eh? It means we're just about home sweet home whenever I gaze upon those lusty mountains."

"We're about there, then? At the reservation?" I wondered how mountains could be lusty but did not bring it up in conversation.

"Mmhmm, but around here, we just call it the rez, short for reserve. But just one stop before we header in, if you don't mind? It's a tradition for me."

"What do you have in mind, mate?" I asked.

"A beer," Tyson brusquely said.

"Alright. I could use a pint."

The bar was called Queens. It was a local hotspot, being one of the only bars in the crossroads town of Fort Macleod. It was unlike the pubs that I was used to back home. I was accustomed to a usual set-up of a sprawling bar table extending down a space that took up a quarter of the pub. My local watering hole back home had a charming, old-timey medieval feeling to it. In contrast, this Queens bar had a small, dingy tabletop bar, with only a few vacant chairs. Most of the patrons were scattered about, sitting around small tables with high-top stools sucked under them. The tiny dance floor was devoid of dancers, but country music blared anyway. Tyson and I found ourselves an empty stall in the back, a few feet from the lone billiards table and coin-operated jukebox.

"Hey, Tyson. Good to see ya bro," a tall man called out. He wore tattered blue jeans with a striped, button-up shirt, a black cowboy hat and a shiny buckled belt wrapped around his waist. I was to learn it was a championship rodeo buckle.

"Oh shit, if ain't my favourite cowboy: Johnny Walker," said Tyson, adding a rude snicker.

"Tsaa, as if, this guy. Don't even start with that, hey," said Johnny. "Mind if I take a seat?" Without a reply, he pulled out a chair and plopped himself down.

Tyson nodded with a smile and turned to me. "You know how he got the name, Johnny Walker?"

I smiled and shook my head.

"Because he spends more time walking in the corral than he does actually riding the damn bull," laughed Tyson, giving the wobbly table a powerful smack.

I smiled and nodded courteously at Tyson's comical remark. I really didn't want to laugh crudely, for fear of angering this six-foot-something bull rider who'd just taken a seat at our table. "Good evening, mate, I'm Paxton. How do you do," I said with an outstretched arm.

"Oh yeah, this is Paxton. My apologies," said Tyson, pausing to clear his throat.

"So, you're an English feller, or something?" said Johnny. He snatched my hand in his and gave it a firm, twisting handshake.

"I am," I said.

"You know, my great-great-grandfather was from Ireland," said Johnny. "Hell, lemme buy you a beer. Hope you English boys like real beer." He got up from his seat and vanished toward the bar without taking in an answer from me.

"Charming lad," I said to Tyson.

"Ahh, don't let his thickness get to ya. He just fell off a few too many bulls and horses is all. Hell, he's prolly even been kicked by a few too many, too," said Tyson.

"What do ya figure? A few beers then be back on our way?" I asked.

"You betcha. I just need a few jiggles of a leg to shake this damn hangover."

There really is no such instance as a few beers. Even back home in England, the old saying is more jibber jabber than fact. I wasn't one to complain that night though. In a matter of no time, our table was full of local Indian cowboys, and they were all more than delighted to buy the foreign Englishman a few rounds. So, I figured I would stay awhile and drink with them and listen to their stories of lives as Indian cowboys.

But good times were never meant to last—especially when the alcohol was flowing freely. It wasn't too far into our evening when a fight broke out between Tyson and Johnny, and it was all over who owned a more powerful truck. Silly, really. Of course, we were tossed out into the parking lot on our arses.

"Come on, I know where there's a party. It's not far from here," slurred Tyson, his breath stained with the reek of Budweiser and whiskey.

"Bloody hell, you're not good to drive, mate," I said, wobbling on my feet more than a little.

"No-o-o, not even, bro. I'm wicked good to go. I just had a few beers is all. Peanuts. Now come on, the girls are waiting on us."

"You know, my cousin once got into a nasty car accident. He too thought he'd only had a few and was good to drive. Bur no, that was not the case. Now he's in a wheelchair for life."

"Well, I'll tell you what. You drive," he said, pointing at me while digging through his pockets with his other hand for his keys.

"Nope, not a good idea, mate. I had a few too many, and besides, I don't have a licence to drive in this country."

"Come on, bro, don't be such a puss. We'll backroad it. Won't even see no cops."

"Still not a good idea," I strongly asserted. But I clearly saw that there would be no persuading him.

"Okay then, how about this. I'll go and pick up the girls, and we'll come back for you."

"Your call," I said reluctantly. I had the distinct feeling Tyson would not be coming back for me. A good hunch as it happened.

"Alright bro. I'll be right back, right quick."

Shaking my head in disapproval, I watched as Tyson drunkenly climbed aboard his raised pickup truck, starting it up and revving it hard, making the motor growl like a wild animal. I then watched a black police cruiser emerge from out of nowhere into the parking lot with a squeal of its tires, cherries and blueberries activated for dramatic effect. Tyson was blocked in.

As much as I felt bad for poor Tyson about to be arrested, I was just glad he didn't get a chance to leave the parking lot behind the wheel—and in the state he was in.

I slipped into the shadows and carried on with my journey.

PART V

THE NIGHT WAS COOL, but the blacktop pavement radiated the day's absorbed summer heat. I headed eastward, strolling casually down what I figured was a deserted Main Street. The roadside side businesses were all interconnected, looking just like iconic buildings from Wild West movies. In less than thirty minutes, I was at the margin of the town, the illumination from street lights dimming into blackness as the onslaught of the wild prairies emerged. I began to stroll when the sudden burst from a police siren from behind made me jump.

"Sir ... a quick minute? ..." asked a voice.

I slowly pivoted on the heels of my boots to face a police officer seated in his cruiser. "Yes, sir, alright."

The police officer commended my smart actions of not getting inside the truck with Tyson, as intoxicated as he was. He asked where I was headed. I told him a quick version of my ancestry hunt and my intended excursion to the Blood Tribe. The reserve was out of his direct jurisdiction, but he offered to drive me to the boundaries, where I could finish my trek, and even be upon the central town site of Standoff in a matter of hours. I happily obliged.

"Alrighty, Mr. Paxton. Just stay on this here road and you should be at Standoff in no time. And if any cars pass by, take extra caution, please. I don't want no fatalities, especially from a person not born of this country," said the police officer.

"Will do, Constable. Thank you again, I certainly appreciate the lift, indeed," I said as I closed the passenger door.

We said our cheerios, and the kind constable departed with a polite honk of his horn, propelling back down the desolate roadway from whence we came. I watched as his red taillights became one with the night like diminishing fireflies. I was once again alone in the darkened wilderness with nothing but the sounds of crickets chirping to keep me company.

I glanced at my wristwatch. 10:42 p.m., July 16, 2008.

Like I said before, I'd been on my own for more instances than I can recall. My fear of anything lurking beyond the cover of backcountry darkness had long since dissipated. Like a daring explorer, I marched on.

Not an hour into my walk, I badly wished that I had asked the constable to make a pit stop at the Mac's store for a bottle of water on the way out of town. The intoxicating effects of my few hours at the bar had disintegrated and I was left with a searing headache along with intense cottonmouth. The dry air of the prairie didn't help matters either.

My paced boot stomps and the buzz of nocturnal critters echoed through the cool night. Before long, an embracing melody of music drifted through the open atmosphere and enveloped my isolated senses. I stopped to have a listen. Still, I couldn't grasp where it was coming from. In the flat, remote distance were spread-out specks of light, what I presumed were separate reserve dwellings and farm acreages. Excitement once again brewed from the pit of my stomach. Water was on my mind. I continued forward with my steady stride. The music gradually grew louder with each set of footstep crunches on the gravel road. I picked up speed until I was almost at a full-tilt run.

At last, I could see a set of lights emerging from a lone building in the distance, like a rising sun, and I caught drifts of people talking and laughing. I smiled, slowed my pace and breathing, and walked towards the light, thinking I might get a smidge of water.

As I approached the lone building, I could see it looked like a broad, old-fashioned church. Two tall streetlamps were positioned on each end of the gravel parking lot, their dull glow dousing the area in a gloomy orange tint. There were at least a dozen people or so standing about in small groups, drinking from bottles and smoking cigarettes. Haphazardly parked cars littered the parking lot. Most of the vehicles looked too ancient to still be on the roads.

As I approached, a group that was outside chatting suddenly fell to dead silence. My footsteps on the gravel sounded eerie, even to me. The group's flickering cigarette cherries along with some dark shadows were the only indications of life. Once again, I could only hear crickets chirping and the ambience of thumping music from within the building. I could feel cold gazes stabbing at me through the already-cool night.

I stepped cautiously forward and called out, "Umm, hello there. I'm sort of lost—I think," I said cautiously.

"Well, well, well. Would ya boys listen to that? Sounds like we got a Scotsman in our midst," said one of the men. I couldn't tell who the speaker was from the shadows enshrouding their faces.

"Uhh, yeah," I giggled uncomfortably. I figured now wasn't the time to correct the man and perhaps upset him—and his group of chums.

"I take it you're lost, eh?" said another man taking a leaping step from the group. "Well tellin' by your accent, you're wickedly lost." He broke out in a fit of laughter. The remaining group of men joined in.

"I am," I said.

They continued laughing at me as I stood motionless.

"Geez, you guys, can't you see he's lost and means us no harm? Now let's show him some hospitality," said a woman's voice. I hadn't noticed her and still couldn't see her face.

"Ehh, we're just teasin' him is all," blurted out a third, unknown man. He stepped out from the group and jogged toward me. At point-blank, he stopped right in front of me to light up a cigarette. The illumination from the lighter flame revealed his facial features. He looked exactly like the Indian men from my schoolbooks: long black hair that sailed past his powerful shoulders and black, almond eyes that looked like they had seen their fair share of skirmishes. Battle scars, I assumed, carved across his left cheek down to his well-formed chin.

My hands were sweaty and my heart hammered but I managed to say, "Hello."

"Oki, tsa niitapi?" he said.

"I beg your pardon?"

He broke out in a friendly chuckle. "I was just saying, hello, how are you?"

"Oh, okay. Another Blackfoot language lesson, then."

"Another?" he asked. In the dim lamplight I could see his black eyebrows rise.

"A fellow I got a ride from spoke Blackfoot," I said.

"Why'd he do that," he asked. I could finally feel the coldness departing from his voice.

"This is the Blood Tribe, right?" I asked.

"It is," said the man standing in front of me.

I replied to this with a bottomless sense of pride, "My great-grandfather was from this reserve."

The tension between us dissipated. "I'm Arthur. That guy is Ramsey, he's from Amskapi Piikuni, our Blackfeet cousins to the south." Arthur gestured to another person still in shadow.

"Chuffed to meet you, Arthur," I said, extending my hand to him.

"You drink?" asked Arthur. He clutched my hand tightly and gave me an unfamiliar hand clasp.

"I would fancy some water, if you would have some?"

"There's prolly some inside. But for now, here, take this," said Ramsey. He shoved his way past the others and handed me a partially cold bottle of Budweiser. "Come on, let's drink," he said with a wide smile. "I've never drank me with no Scotsman."

I felt that I had warmed up enough to these gentlemen to politely correct him. "Actually, Ramsey, I'm from England."

"Oh okay, my apologies. So you said your grandpa was from here? What was his name?" asked Ramsey. Like Arthur, his long black hair was tied in a tidy ponytail.

In no time, I was acquainted with the group of people standing outside. I was surrounded like a pack of wolves closing in for the kill. Only this pack didn't have eradication on their minds. They lined up and took turns stepping up to me and introducing themselves.

Most of them had never once seen a foreign man step foot on the reserve lands—let alone share a beer with one. I was the centre of attention.

Following a few unfamiliar, odd-tasting drinks, Arthur offered to take me inside to meet more people and even some of their Elders. I was informed that the occasion for the gathering was a wedding, a lively old merriment.

The wide-open, gymnasium-like interior was dimly lit. Candles, which had been placed upright in the centre of an arrangement of round tables, danced and flickered. Colourful banners and traditional Indigenous designs adorned the corners of the four walls. A lively band strummed their guitars and banged on a drum kit while the singer covered classic rock songs that I knew had been popular back in the day. Ramsey chaperoned me around the different tables of guests.

I met a handful of couples and relatives—old and young alike. Each one was thrilled to hear that my great-grandfather was of their very own lineage. Some of the guests steered clear of me, gazing at me with rigidness, like I was a foreign animal in their domain. In a way I was. From my studies I knew about the hardships suffered by Indigenous Peoples as a result of French, then British colonization. I asked about kids and was told that there were no children in attendance due to the presence of alcohol. Fair enough.

Lastly, I was brought to the table reserved for the Elders. Some had their hair in braids and others wore swanky fedoras and cowboy hats. I was honoured to meet and greet such people who could trace their experience and family customs and ceremonies back to the early, traditional ways of life. They were just as thrilled to meet me. One of the older men told me he may have even fought in the same regiment as my great-grandfather. I felt privileged.

"Well, that should be about everybody, I'd say," said Arthur, showing me through to the brightly lit kitchen.

"I can't begin to thank you enough for welcoming me in. This is definitely one of the highlights of my trip thus far," I said.

"Man, don't even worry about it. It's our privilege, bro. Hell it's not every day that we get to come across a real-life Englishman."

I raised my glass and Arthur lightly tapped it from top to bottom.

I carried on through the night, drinking and exchanging stories with the people. In no time, my mind slipped from my full grasp on perception and into the blackened world of intoxication.

WHEN I OPENED MY EYES, I was in near-total darkness, minus the strips of dusty sunlight piercing into the room through the cracked margins of boarded-up windows. My blistered taste buds were swamped in a viscous taste of copper mingled with stale alcohol. Once again, I severely needed water.

I pushed off the stiff sofa I was sprawled across. A foul spray of dust and dirt exploded and hovered in the air, forcing me into a fit of coughing. I sat up to let my blurred eyes unite with my battered conscience. Wide awake, I stood up and immediately fell back down with shock. The room I was in was old. In fact, it was beyond old. It conveyed the look of countless years immersed in abandonment. The walls were tattered and broken, revealing crumbling drywall and inner studs of rotting wood. The floor was swathed in layers of grime, mould, and black muck.

I glanced at my watch. 11:07 a.m. July 17, 2008.

Had I dreamt my night of fun? I couldn't have. I could still taste the sour traces of the potent liquor I had pounded back with my new friends, Arthur and Ramsay.

I stumbled through an open door to a darkened bathroom and lunged for it. I tried the faucets. They were tightly rusted in place, emitting a loud squeal as I twisted them with all my strength. Nothing came out. I tried the light switch. Nothing. Even the mirror I stared at was caked in years of grime and dust buildup.

Then I remembered my pack. I burst out of the bathroom and raked my head around the dusty room. My pack was nowhere to be seen. Panic arose in me like a gasoline-doused fire. I pushed my way through the double doors I remembered Arthur and Ramsey ushering me through last night. The doors swivelled strenuously on creaky, rusted hinges. It felt like they hadn't been used in years.

Out of the back kitchen, I recognized where I was. There were no intricate Indigenous designs and decorative banners embellishing the hall. Only marred, brick-constructed walls stood upright with smears of black char and other unknown filth. Neatly organized tables were no longer in existence, replaced by heaps of burnt rubble and furniture remains. The large, open ballroom was dark except for puffs of dust glittering in light beams trickling in through scores of holes in the dilapidated roof like mini spotlights. The air was thick with the choking aroma of burnt wood and aged char.

I wasted no time and sprinted across the grand room toward the front entrance. From behind me I could still sense the coldness of unseen eyes gazing right through me. Like a crazed escapee, I burst out the front entrance doors and was immediately blinded by the downpour of the high-summer sun. Taking a few steps further away, I shielded my eyes and scanned the flat, grassy horizon. In the distance of wind-dancing grasses, I could see the movement of cars on a highway, progressing like small insects.

One last glance behind me, and I was off like a bat out of hell. The very sight of the charred remains of the building gave me gooseflesh. I ignored the searing desiccation in my throat and kept my legs moving until I felt I was well and safe enough away from the forsaken building.

And then I saw it.

My eyes lit up like an explorer stumbling upon gold. There was my pack, sitting upright at the edge of the gravel road, half concealed by tall stalks of prairie grass. I snatched it up without stopping and bolted toward the T-intersection where the gravel met the blacktop. Once my boots touched pavement, I stopped and unshouldered my bag. I always came prepared. Fishing through my pack, I seized my compass and headed southeast. It wasn't too long before another Good Samaritan pulled off onto the shoulder and politely tooted their horn.

"That thing looks heavy. Come on, you look like you can use a lift," said the driver, a lively young man. I knew he was a local from his acute, and now much familiarized, accent and tanned skin.

I tossed my pack into the cargo box and climbed into the man's truck. "Thank you so much, mate," I said, my voice a little gravelly.

He gave me a once-over before slamming on the accelerator. "What'd you camp out in the boonies or something?"

"It's a long story. And you probably wouldn't believe me if I told you," I said.

"Try me," he chuckled. "I've heard 'em all."

I disclosed my full story of the strange night I had unexpectedly encountered. I left out no details of the alcohol I had consumed and the tangible people I had graciously met. By the time I was done my story, the driver stared at me with his mouth fully agape. The tanned colour from his face dissipated into a milky whiteness.

"That old community hall. What I am about to tell you...." He paused to take a deep breath and exhale. "There was a fire there, some thirty years ago. It was supposed to be a grand celebration of two long-time lovers finally tying the knot. And then a very stupid prank by one of the bride's younger brothers went wrong. The fire killed many people that night."

"Wait a minute. So what you're saying is that I was having a merry old time ... with a gathering of ghosts?" I said with my face twisting in repugnance.

The driver glanced over at me with graveness reeling in his eyes. "My friend, you're not the first and almost certainly you won't be the last."

∼ FIVE ∼

SPOOKED

THE REMAND CENTRE stood on the farmland and wild prairie outskirts of the sprawling city, directly across a narrow, two-lane service road from a massive construction site. The sign pointing to the opposite side of the remand centre's branch of paved road read: Future Home of Canary Laboratory Services.

Lab services, the man thought. *Who in their right mind would ever want to build a lab next to a jail?* He cornered the turnoff hard and came to a tire-screeching halt as he parked his Porsche in the visitor's overflow lot. The other visitors' outdated vehicles looked like they were on the last legs of their life journeys.

Shawn Tegan checked his cellphone one more time, tossed it into the glove box, and slowly got out of the form-fitting racing seat. The cool, mountain-borne breeze bit hard at his sweat-dampened skin through his silk dress shirt. He wasn't at all outfitted for the chilly weather. It was August and still supposed to be summer.

As an attorney, he was authorized to skip most of the necessary security inspections that regular visitors had to go through. An X-ray conveyor for his briefcase and other possessions and a metal detector archway were his only security checkpoint measures.

"Hello, Counsellor. How are we today?" asked the correctional officer stationed on the opposite side of the clear, tempered-plastic barrier.

"Not too shabby, Mr. Jamieson. Just another day, another few dollars," replied Tegan.

C.O. Jamieson feigned a smile and keyed the radio resting on his shoulder lapel. "Control, can I get entrance A-2 gate, please."

A loud mechanical buzz along with the sounds of unlatching deadbolts ensued, followed by the C.O. politely opening the heavy, steel-framed door. "So, which one of these law-breaking ingrates are you here to see?" Jamieson asked.

"Innocent until proven guilty," replied Tegan, with a pistol-pointing finger gesture and click of his tongue.

Jamieson scoffed as he picked up the lawyer's briefcase from the conveyor belt and handed it to him.

"I'm here this evening to see Mr. Axel Plume."

C.O. Jamieson looked up, and the lawyer knew he had something to say.

"You know him?" Tegan asked.

"Sure do. I mean his story was in the papers and news and all. But—" He hesitated.

"Go on,"

"Well, if he's guilty of what they say he did, then he sure as hell belongs locked up tightly in this shithole. But then again, he really doesn't seem to be the kind of guy who belongs here."

"You've met the guy?"

"You'll see what I mean." Jamieson waved the lawyer to follow him as a secondary C.O. stepped to man the security desk.

The lawyer and guard marched through a maze of blandly painted brick corridors, stopping three times at unmanned security checkpoints, where Jamieson would have to radio main control to open the steel doors.

While they waited for the final door to be buzzed open, Jamieson faced Tegan. "Welcome to the remand centre, right?"

The lawyer snickered as the door buzzed and clanked open.

"Okay, Mr. Tegan, you'll be in consultation booth three." He pointed to the only glass-encased booth with an open, heavy steel door. "You know what to do. Just give us the signal when you're done, and we'll get you outta here," he said.

Tegan sat in the uncomfortable plastic seat and glanced at his Rolex—one of many lavish gifts to himself following his first successful year with his father's firm. The gold-leaf hands pointed to 6:42 p.m. He wanted to make this interview fast, as it was his final prospective client to meet with. A decent payday and his fifteen minutes of fame was in store for him if he agreed to take the kid's case.

Not three minutes later, Jamieson and a female C.O. returned with the inmate: a tall young man with a slim, athletic build. He waddled like a duck due to the thick, jingling shackles binding his ankles. The two guards brought him into the meeting room that was no larger than the average bathroom and helped him sit in the small seat secured to the concrete floor. Jamieson lingered, appearing as though he was waiting to be given a tip.

"Thank you, Jamieson. I'll take it from here," Tegan said.

Jamieson shot the inmate a sharp look. "Now you be a good boy, ya hear? This guy is one of the best, and he's here to help you. And by the looks of things, you'll need all the help you can get." The inmate smiled half-heartedly. Jamieson winked at Tegan before sealing the heavy door shut, leaving the inmate and lawyer to talk in peace.

Tegan took a moment to scrutinize his prospective client. The kid couldn't have been older than twenty-five. His dark, almost-black hair, fashioned into a faux hawk, gleamed in the fluorescent lighting. His unblemished skin radiated with the slightest tan; he could be either white or Latino.

Tegan had represented his fair share of lowlife, no-good law breakers. His immediate impression of this kid was he didn't seem criminalized.

"Hello, Mr. Plume, did I say it right?" said Tegan.

"You did. But if you want, you can just call me Axe— or Axel if you prefer," he said.

"Axel it is then. Hey, do you like Guns N' Roses?"

A delicate smile began to form on Axel's youthful face, his only reply to the lawyer's question.

"Ahh, I thought so. I'm a big fan," Tegan said.

"My mother actually named me after the lead singer. You believe that shit?"

Tegan grinned. "I could believe it. Heck, she could've named you Slash."

Axel bowed his head, his smile slowly dissipating

as he tried to make himself comfortable on the stiff, unmoving stool. Once finished squirming, he sat quiet and attentive behind his side of the interview table, interlocking his slightly shaking fingers.

The lawyer had seen his fair share of the shaking fingers. "Okay, now, let's get down to business. My name is Shawn Tegan, and I am a lawyer—as you can probably already tell. I was contacted by your mother and stepfather to act as your legal representative. They paid a retainer fee for me to come here and consult with you. You with me so far?"

Axel nodded. "Yeah, that and a friend told me about you."

"Okay. And did your friend happen to tell you how much I charge?"

"Minimum twenty grand?" Axel said, more of a rhetorical question.

"That's correct. I'm not cheap, but I get shit done—"

"I've already told my parents they can sell my car to pay you," interrupted Axel.

"Sorry. Car?"

"I own a '99 Nissan Skyline RB34. Done up to the max." Axel looked down and furrowed his lips. "Selling that should give me enough to pay you."

Tegan had represented his fair share of lowlife, no-good law breakers. His immediate first impression of this kid was that he truly didn't belong where he currently sat. The kid didn't seem criminalized; he seemed normal. He knew he had to hear this kid's story. "Wow. Damn, I hate to deprive a kid of his prized car," he said.

"So, have you heard about what I'm in for?" asked Axel, changing the subject.

Tegan sat up straight and cleared his throat. "I have, yes. Your case was well publicized."

"So, everybody probably knows about it?"

Tegan nodded yes.

Axel cringed. "Damn, that's ... that's crazy. Do you think I'm crazy?" he asked, his brown eyes boring into the lawyer's.

"Well, that's why I'm here. You know I once had a case similar to yours, and—"

"You got him off scot-free?" Axel asked abruptly, his eyes shining with bright hope.

"Not exactly. But first things first. I'm going to have to ask you to give me your statement. A firsthand account. Because your charge is very serious, I need to know what I'm working with here. Can you do that? And then we can go from there."

Axel struggled again to get comfortable atop the small, stationary stool, all the while performing his own assessment of the tall, fair-skinned lawyer with a fit physique. The young lawyer's style was incredibly well-matched with his custom-tailored suit and bald head—a hard look to pull off, but he achieved it well. Letting his guard down after a moment of close scrutiny, Axel decided he would trust the lawyer. "Yeah, I can do that."

Tegan broke out the pen and paper pad, locking his attention on the young man opposite.

I TOOK CARE OF MY GRANDFATHER in the last two years of his life, sacrificing the assistant foreman's job I had through my electricians' apprenticeship. I wasn't upset about derailing my career— to be honest, I was thrilled to be going back home so I could live it up on the reserve. Country life. Reserve life to many means a dull and boring life, but not to me.

Papa, as we called him, was a champion saddle-bronc rider who rode in rodeos all across the USA,

Canada, Central and South America, and even Australia. Money wasn't a big issue for him. He had lots of savings, so I didn't need my construction job anymore while I cared for him. Papa owned pastureland on the southwestern edge of the reserve, looking toward the towers of Rocky Mountains. It was a ranch he inherited from his father. Grandmother passed eleven years ago from cancer, so Papa lived alone.

Papa ultimately got sick; a life of hard drinking and years of pummeling his body in the rodeo corral finally caught up with him. In years long past—it was over a hundred years since the old ranch house belonged to the reserve's Indian Agent—the people who lived on the ranch planted a massive number of trees which became towering spruce and fir. The grounds looked like a small woodland oasis, smack dab in the middle of the rolling, prairie foothills. The old house was near an abandoned residential school and was down the hill from one of the reserve's four cemeteries. Many of our family members believed that being so near to such powerful places meant that there were lots of restless souls lingering about. That part could have been true, but I'd never experienced anything even remotely supernatural.

IN TIME, Papa left us to be with the Creator, and I was left to watch over the house and take care of the ranch on my own. It was something I was already well qualified to do. I was expecting my girlfriend, Brea, to come for a weekend and take me back into town where my pickup truck was being serviced by the local mechanic. I hadn't gotten around to getting a landline hooked up, and the foothills in the area wreaked havoc with cellphone reception. I had talked to Brea earlier, but she had a habit of being late.

Late on a Friday evening, the midsummer sun was just beginning to dip behind the mountains, its rose gold radiance hovering in the wake of pitch-black serrated summits. It was lonely out there but I wasn't totally alone. Even though the horses had been moved to my uncle's nearby ranch, I still had two loyal dogs: Shep and Goose. Shep was a German Shepherd, and Goose was an Alaskan Husky I had rescued from the pound. Shep was a gift from my sister before I moved down to the reserve. She had rescued him just after his early retirement from the police force. Goose was four, and Shep was eight.

I went ahead and ate dinner, thinking that Brea had most likely already stopped somewhere to grab some groceries. I was finishing the dishes when I looked out the window and spotted the unmistakable glint of headlights journeying along the long, narrow road up over a steep hill that joined the ranch to the main highway on the other side.

I checked my watch: 9:58 p.m.

I hadn't seen Brea in two long weeks, and I was excited for her arrival. I called the dogs and escaped the house, making my way down the twisting driveway. The summer heat still clung to the evening, its warmth radiating from the gravel. A crescent half-moon emerged in the sky as the dogs and I walked down the road. I waited patiently at the Texas gate entrance while the speeding car slowed to a crawl.

No dice. It didn't sound like Brea's Jeep. The dogs even became anxious, probably knowing better than I did that this visitor was unsolicited.

"Now, now. Shep, Goose, you guys' just chill, alright?" I ordered them.

The car slowed further some twenty feet ahead, leaving its headlights fixed on me. I was nervous but I kept my composure and slowly backed up, not wanting to look surprised or caught off guard.

"Hey asshole," a hoarse male voice said from inside the vehicle, followed by a woman's giggle.

"Who are you? This is private property."

The only sound that followed was the car's fan struggling to keep the engine cool.

"I know that, asshole. What are you doing out here all alone, besides the two mutts? Lemme guess, someone supposed to come and visit your lonesome ass?" the male said, his snort echoed once again by giggles from the female passenger.

Drunks, I thought. Nothing but drunks. There was no shortage of these guys prowling around on a Friday night around the reserve. Sometimes there was nothing better to do. I shuttered at the idea of a confrontation and decided to turn around and walk home before I got myself into trouble.

"Okay, asshole, I was gonna give you a ride—but nope. Not anymore. I guess I'll just meet you at the house, then." With that, I recognized the sound of the transmission gears being engaged before the car's stereo was dialed up to full blast. The vehicle lurched violently forward, churning up a wake of dust lights. The car raced past me—ignoring the jarring Texas gate lattices—leaving me choking on gravel dust and exhaust.

I ran after the car, not knowing what kind of outcome to expect once I confronted these people. I moved into the high prairie grasses to get out of the billowing trail of dust and decided I would flank the vehicle, knowing all too well that they would be expecting me to come from directly behind them. Like a swift fox, I skulked through the undergrowth and trees, keeping my body hunched low and my head fixed toward the unwanted intruders.

The dogs did likewise, as I had trained them to do on our hunting excursions.

Our Blackfoot reserve is known to be full of a lot of crazies. Crazies that had nothing better to do on a weekend than go and terrorize a helpless family—or a lone man in this case. I stooped until my head was level with the tops of the spear grass. I focused hard, seeing that the car was parked, the occupants still inside. For all I knew, there could have easily been three—maybe four more crazies crammed into the back seats, an Indian squeeze.

The driver finally slid out of the front seat. "Where'd he go?" this guy asked, sounding concerned. "I swear he was just right behind us."

"You probably scared him off," laughed the girl. She got out of the vehicle, and together they looked around for me.

I stood my ground, waiting another few minutes in my grassy cover until I realized no one else was in the car.

"Alright, you two," I whispered to the dogs, "stay on me." I lunged out of the grass toward the two car occupants. "I'm right here. What the hell do you want from me?" My hands balled up into fists, and I could feel my untrimmed fingernails burrowing into my palms.

"Whoa, whoa, chill, cuz! I just came to visit you is all," said the man. I finally recognized his voice.

"Damien?" I asked. The faces of the now-familiar man and the unknown girl were in silhouette from the porch light at their backs.

"Yeah. What, you too cool to hang with your ol' cousin, or what?" Damien said.

Damien, my cousin, had tormented me as a child. For years his name ignited fear and hatred in my heart until I was able to stand up to him. That had been a good day, and Damien had shown me respect ever since.

"I'm never too cool for that, man. How are you?" I asked. I hadn't seen Damien in almost three years. He hadn't even shown up to Papa's funeral.

"Came to have a drink with you, Mr. Axe-man," said Damien, brandishing a bottle.

"Uhh, well, I"—I hesitated—"I'm kind of waiting on my—"

"Come on, bro. It's been what, three years? And I want you to meet my new girlfriend."

That was a laugh and a half. This guy went through girlfriends like I did sneakers. "Ah, fine then," I said. "I guess. Go on in. The door's unlocked." He introduced his girlfriend Dani, and we made an impromptu tour of the house I'd been redecorating.

"So, how's Papa's house been treatin' ya these days?" asked Damien, his eyes darting around the spacious sitting room.

"Well, I've been keeping her clean and whatnot, you know, the basics. When I redid the electrical wiring, my J-Man ticket came in handy," I said.

"Wow, this is, like, a really nice house. And it's so much more spacious in here than it looks from the outside," said Dani, wide-eyed.

Damien was slugging back a drink from the bottle of cognac when he shot Dani a sharp look.

"Yeah, I took down a few walls to make it more spacey. And a little more custom redecorating—with the girlfriend's help that is," I said proudly.

"So, you're dating a white girl now, huh?" Damien cut in, wiping his lips. I sat quiet and still. My fists began curling into balls again.

"Wow, that's amazing. I wish someone would do

stuff like that for *our* house," Dani said.

"Hey, wait a minute," Damien grunted, his ego obviously damaged. "You've never asked me to fix up house."

"Should I really have to?" snapped Dani. She was pretty. Almost too pretty for the likes of Damien, who sat choking on stifled comebacks.

I was beginning to think there was about to be a domestic dispute, breaking the serenity of my living room. I knew I had to change the subject—and fast. "So, you two live together? How long you been going out?" I asked.

Dani pushed off the leather loveseat and got to her feet, sighing heavily. She walked across the room and eyed a painting that faced the living room's curtain-covered window.

Damien's eyes tracked her movement before falling back on me. "Just over a year now."

"Nice. Where'd ya two meet?" I asked. "If you don't mind my asking."

Damien put his index finger in the air and reached for the bottle of cognac. He took a stiff shot and handed me the bottle.

I brought the bottle's neck close to my nose. "You know this stuff is pretty potent for my taste. I'm more of a beer guy. Is there any chaser that goes good with this stuff?"

"Coke will most likely do best. Or no, Dr. Pepper," said Dani, her back to me.

"Yes, that'll work. I have just the stuff." I got to my feet and headed for the kitchen.

While I ransacked my fridge for some Coke, I eavesdropped. I heard Damien attempting to cheer Dani up. It made me miss Brea.

I went back into the sitting room where Damien and

Dani were snuggling on the leather loveseat. I smiled. "No Coke in the fridge. I'm gonna go down to the basement pantry and grab some of the warm ones."

"Want me to roll with?" asked Damien.

"No, no, you two look comfortable. I'll only be like thirty seconds."

"I dunno, man. I think I should join ya. Especially after what happened to me down there."

My eyebrows shot up. "Say what, now?" I knew Damien was full of ghost stories he'd supposedly heard.

Damien cleared his throat. "Better have a seat and have a shot. Cause I'm about to scare your socks off."

As much as I frowned on the bulk of Damien's logical abilities, I always thought he should have become a writer with all the frightening tales he knew—both fact and fiction. I was ready for some entertainment.

The warm Coke would wait.

I took a seat in the recliner across from them, snatched the bottle from the table, and knocked back a stiff one. I immediately regretted it, as the auburn firewater burned like a vat of spilled acid. "Holy, hot damn. How can ya drink this stuff straight?" I croaked.

Damien grinned at me slyly. That grin used to strike fear into my heart. "You ready?" he asked.

"Okay. Let's hear it," I said.

"Okay then, but first." Damien reached into his chest pocket and brandished a joint the size of a thick caterpillar.

"Now that, I could do," I said.

Damien's story was about how he supposedly came over to visit Papa after a night of heavy drinking. Of course, Papa had a big heart so he got out of bed, opened the door, and let him in, telling him he could crash downstairs. Damien stumbled down to the basement and immediately passed out. Sometime during the middle of the night, he was violently awakened—by something unseen in the darkness. Blaming his liquor-triggered headache, he got up to cool off his hungover head in the downstairs bathroom.

Damien took a few sips of water and returned to the bedroom. His dazed head was swimming. Papa's private study, with one solitary desk and chair perched below a high window, sat between the bathroom and the spare bedroom. From the light of the moon seeping in, Damien thought he saw someone sitting at the desk. He figured it was Papa, sitting and having a late-night cigarette, as he never smoked upstairs.

Back in bed, Damien's eyelids were slowly getting heavy when he saw a figure enter the roomy, like a spooked cat running for safety. "Papa?" he asked. He heard something moving on the far side of the room. Damien got out of bed and went to investigate.

The guest room was big, with a handmade blanket acting as a partition in the middle of the room and another writing desk on the opposite side of the blanket.

Damien swept aside the makeshift curtain and gasped. A black figure, hunched over the desk, with eyes like burning red coals, stared back at him. It rose to its feet. Standing tall, its head almost touched the ceiling.

Damien bolted up the stairs and out to his car, not bothering to wake up Papa.

"Is that it?" I asked, yawning. I politely covered my mouth. The lingering weed smoke tickled my tired eyes.

I checked my watch: 10:48 p.m. Damien's story had taken a lot longer to disclose than necessary. I had already heard the story before—once or twice. I remember them both being told by a drunken Damien, never sober.

"Yeah," Damien said.

"You told me the story different last time," Dani said, eyes half closed.

Damien managed a weak smile before grasping the bottle and slamming back another stiff shot. "It's true." He grimaced. "But you have to remember, I was still pretty buzzed when I woke up, so the actual account is kinda hazy." He handed me the cognac.

I scrutinized the bottle carefully, not taking it in my hand. "Well, I'm going to go downstairs and get those Cokes now, so excuse me." I got unsteadily to my feet and hurried out of the room before Damien had a chance to say something asinine.

Too late.

"Don't get spooked now. Oooooooh," he hooted and snickered drunkenly.

"Oh you, you're such an ass," scolded Dani. I was starting to like her. What Damien really needed was a good girl to put him in his place when the time called.

I flicked the basement light on. I hadn't gotten around to installing fluorescent lighting in the basement. The sixty-watt bulb sputtered to life, bathing the timeworn staircase in a disconcerting orange glow. The stairs creaked and groaned as I descended—a sound that always put me on edge. The six-pack of soda was on the top shelf of the custom-wooden pantry. I grabbed them and headed back upstairs.

But first, sheer curiosity got the best of me.

I made my way to the bathroom, wanting to trace the footsteps that Damien would have taken in his horror story. I turned on the bathroom light and admired my renovation job for a second before turning the light back off, leaving me in darkness. Casually, I strolled through the basement toward the guest room, slowing as I walked by Papa's study, its door wide open.

I peeked inside.

Nothing. Of course.

Papa's writing desk was still huddled beneath the window, as empty as the bathroom I had just come from.

Next was the guest room. It was cold— cold air was seeping into the room. Next, I examined the window high on the wall. Sure enough, a thin twig was jammed in between the window frame and the sturdy sill. It happened all the time, especially from the overgrowth of untrimmed bushes and hedges circling the foundation. I climbed on a chair, removed the twig, locked the window, and hurried back upstairs.

"Found 'em," I said, brandishing the pack of cola.

"Mmmm, my favourite. May I?" Dani asked politely.

"Yes, you may." I yanked a lukewarm can from the plastic and handed it to her. "How about you?" I asked Damien.

His drunken, half-closed eyes slid toward me. "Naaw, I'm—I'm good. I was just gonna go and—yeah, no, I'm good, bro," he slurred.

"Did you drink anymore while I was gone?" I asked.

"He did. He downed, like, three huge shots while you were downstairs," Dani said, half angry and half amused. I glanced at the bottle of cognac. About two fingers of the bronze liquid rested at the bottom of the fancy bottle.

"Rest is yours, man," Damien said.

Again, I glanced at my watch. "You know, I think I'm going to get a head start on some sleep. I gotta head up the hill first thing in the morning to call Brea, then run into town to do some errands."

"Yeah, that sounds good. We should get going," affirmed Dani, her voice now void of all amusement. "Come on, Dame, let's get going."

Dame. I had never heard that one before.

"Alright, brother. I'm gonna letchu sleep now. You have to see your white girlfriend, wife chick." Damien tried to get to his feet on his own and fell back to the couch with a recoiling bounce. "I'm wasted," he laughed.

IT TOOK OVER TEN MINUTES for Dani and me to get Damien from the living room and into their beater of a car. The worst of it was trying to squeeze him into the small passenger seat. He was out cold, snoring away before I even closed the passenger door.

I waited until Dani was comfortably in the car before walking back up the stairs to the house. "Wait," she yelled at me over the ear-piercing screech of their car's struggling fan belt.

I stopped midway up the staircase and turned around. "Yeah?"

"Just to let you know," she started, "what he really wanted to come over for was to tell you why he wasn't at your grandfather's funeral."

"Oh, really?" I was curious.

"Yeah, really," she echoed. "But it's not any of my business to say, so I'll remind him tomorrow and give him shit for getting so drunk on you."

I was really starting to like Dani. "Yeah, no worries, it's nothing. It's Damien, after all," I teased.

She giggled and waved. "Yeah. Okay, have a good night," she said as she backed up and turned the car around.

"You too." I returned the wave, watching as the tail-lights twisted down the driveway and waned down the road, disappearing behind a cloud of black dust.

"I wonder what his excuse was going to be this time,"

I wondered out loud. "I guess I'll find out tomorrow."

I wasn't really tired; mostly I'd just wanted to get the drunken Damien out of my hair. I lay down on the couch and thought about Brea. My eyes closed. I was beginning to worry about her.

It wasn't long before I felt like I was being watched. I opened my eyes to catch Shep and Goose sitting on their tails, eyeing me. They had been hiding in my bedroom the whole time. Maybe they sensed Damien's not-so-goodness.

"You know, you two staring at me like that ain't making me feel any better. Thanks, jerks," I said with a snicker. "Bathroom?" I said in a playful tone.

I twisted the rusty handle to the outer screen door. I hated the squealing sound it made, but replacing doors was never my thing. Cool air slapped me in the cheeks and bit at my exposed arms as I stepped out onto the huge, dark patio porch. I kept the porch light off and watched as Shep and Goose stampeded down the wooden steps and galloped off into the moon-shimmering grass, playfully nipping at each other's tails. "Now, you two take your time. I'll be back for you in five minutes." I turned and went back inside, shivering from the sudden breath of cold mountain air.

I plopped back down on the leather couch, my eyes wandering towards the bottle of cognac. Dare I? I pondered. Now that Damien was gone, I felt like slugging back a few more shots. I turned on some music and checked my messages; Brea's Facebook status said she was offline. No surprise there, as she wasn't the sort of person to text and drive. The cola did a good job of masking the potent aftertaste of cognac. Before I could even realize how much I had drunk, all that remained in the bottle of the brown liquid was a slight drizzle—spider, as we called it back home. I wasn't much of a drinker, but I sure welcomed the anaesthetic feeling brought on by the cognac that night. Suddenly, I wasn't too worried about Brea. I knew that she would have a valid reason for not showing up.

Five minutes turned into twenty-five.

"Oh shit, the dogs," I said, my tongue half numb and slurring over my words. "I'm drunk," I laughed, a satisfying head rush slamming me as I sat up. I had lost track of time, scrolling, too busy living vicariously through my friends' Friday night Facebook posts.

I glanced at my watch: 11:39 p.m.

I got to my feet, feeling the warmth of thickened blood rush to my head. That part I disliked. Wobbling slightly, I entered the kitchen, grabbed my windbreaker, and turned on the porch light.

The cool breeze felt good. It's amazing how quickly a warm night turns ice cold, even in the middle of summer.

"Shep, G-o-o-o-ose? Come on boys—it's time to come inside."

Nothing.

I called again, "Shep, Goose, hurry the hell up. It's cold out here." I listened acutely, trying to not sway on my feet.

No mini stampede of their eager footsteps. No furry bodies bounding through the grass. None of Goose's endless barking. It wasn't unlike the dogs to go out and explore the countryside on their own, but it was very unlike them to do it in the dead of the night. My buzz was suddenly halted and replaced with adrenaline and the overwhelming sense of alarm.

I dashed inside and pulled open my junk drawer in search of a flashlight. I found one stashed in the very back. With light in hand, I went back out to the patio and scanned the immediate area in the front and back of the house.

Still no sign of the dogs.

The temperature outside took a drastic nosedive, feeling like an October night rather than August. I ran down to the basement and ransacked my winter and fall clothing. A large woollen jacket buried beneath the clothing stacks was the first one I found. I donned it like a knight's armour. As I clambered back up the stairs, my drunk—but still keen—hearing picked up on movement from somewhere beyond a number of stacked boxes. I froze partway up the creaky stairs, my wide eyes peering through the dim 60W light.

"It's just Damien's stories getting to you," I reassured myself. Seeing and hearing nothing further, I picked up my pace and took the remaining stairs two at a time, bursting out the front door.

In no time, my white tennis shoes became heavily soiled from the dusty roads and waist-high grasses. I searched the grounds relentlessly on foot with flashlight blazing through the darkness until, at last, I came upon the abandoned road leading up to the old residential school. A large, dilapidated sign stood at a broken angle, charred in some spots: Welcome to Mountview Residential School.

Nope, no dogs.

Shadows stalked me like bad spirits until I felt I was well enough away from the forsaken residential school. I hated living so close to that damned building. Even during daylight hours, when coming within proximity of the grounds, I could sense the lingering effects of the pain my ancestors had endured within that heinous structure. The darkness began to weigh heavy on

When coming within proximity of the grounds, I could sense the lingering effects of the pain my ancestors had endured within that heinous structure.

my thoughts, so I decided to wait until morning to find the dogs. I headed back home and figured I would call up Uncle Gunny and we would both go on horseback in search of them tomorrow.

Sleep eluded me as I lay awake in my bed. I couldn't stop worrying about the dogs. Finally, I rolled out of bed. I hadn't been away from the dogs for a night since I got them.

SMASH!

I was jolted fully alert; the sound had come from

beneath the floorboards right where I was sitting. It sounded like one of the jars of preserves had fallen off the shelf of the pantry. But who—or what—was down there?

I rose from the armchair and tiptoed to my bedroom. Kneeling in the dark, I fished under my bed and carefully slid out the .308 Winchester. It was dark, and I was a little drunk and very worried, and was starting to believe that something had ventured down, either from the graveyard or from the deserted residential school and had decided to give me the scare of a lifetime.

Mission accomplished.

I was terrified.

Firearms would do absolutely nothing against a malevolent spirit. But still, just having my hunting rifle in hand gave me an extra sense of security. What if it wasn't a ghost, but just some intoxicated crazy breaking in? This wasn't Texas. I could still get in loads of trouble for shooting an intruder, but this was my house. That's what lawyers are for.

Flashlight duct-taped to my rifle barrel, I cautiously moved down the basement stairs, sweeping the powerful beam ahead of my path like a landmine detector. I made it to the cement landing after seemingly endless minutes of careful footsteps. The concrete was ice-cold, and again I had the sensation of a draft trickling in from somewhere. I wanted to call out that I was armed, but I chose not to. I didn't want my voice sailing off into the unknown.

As the flashlight beam swept across the emptiness, the basement seemed unnervingly bigger, like I was staring into an unfamiliar cavern. A dark, asymmetrical cavern. Maybe it was the weed. Maybe it was the cognac. Perhaps it was both, taking their turns to taunt my stormy imagination. I blinked hard a few times and took a moment to seal my eyes shut, saying a little silent prayer in my head. Then I opened my eyes. The basement was back to its regular state of dimness with mountains of ancient boxes stacked about.

The windows of the basement bedroom and study were my first stop. They were locked tight. Next, I stopped at the pantry. A large jar of pickles and my auntie's homemade raspberry jam were shattered in unpleasant heaps on the floor.

"What the shit?" I grumbled. There was no way the two jars could have been moved by a mouse. It would have taken a much larger animal: a cat or even a raccoon to dislodge them from the sturdy pantry shelf. I owned no cat, and the closed windows barred any other animal.

"Eff this, I'm going back upstairs." Like a vanguard soldier guarding the rear, I skulked backwards, keeping the rifle barrel and flashlight beam directed to my wake. On my ascent, the basement once again turned to that unfamiliar cave, with large, dark cavities forming. Perfect for hiding intruders.

Once upstairs, I was able to focus on slowing my heavy breathing and racing heart. I wished I had some more of the cognac to soothe my battered nerves. Damien had probably left some splendid green, or at least a sizeable roach. I rushed to where he had been sitting and rummaged through the stack of papers and Damien's ashtray. My hands were shaking. After what felt like forever, I found what I was looking for. I rolled a pinner and smoked to my heart's content.

Nerves stimulated by this sativa, I laid back and closed my eyes, thinking good thoughts in order to take my mind off of an unaccounted-for girlfriend, two missing dogs, and a ghost lurking in my basement. With music playing quietly, my eyelids began feeling heavy. At last. Good. I was just dozing off when round two started.

SMASH!

Again, I was torn from my relaxed state of mind, my breath coming in painful gasps. In the blink of an eye, I was seated upright. My feet shifted and were about to hit the floor when I heard the bloodcurdling sound of something charging up the basement stairs. At the same time, a clawing sound came from the front door. I was out of the comfortable leather couch and bounding down the hallway towards the backdoor in another blink, scooping up my rifle and shouldering it. Just as my hand reached for the rear door handle, I stopped and turned to face the open hallway. I had to know. I peered down the corridor, nearly jumping out of my skin when my bedroom door swung open with a loud bang.

I dove out the screen door and bowled into a tumbling somersault down the small set of raggedy wooden stairs. Ignoring the searing pain in my ribs and shoulders, I checked my rifle. It was good. Keeping the flashlight off, I dashed for the nearest trees.

While I remained in the tangle of overgrowth, I watched my partially lit up homestead windows. Minutes passed, and I was about to head back to the house when I saw a black shadow whiz by the large rectangular sitting room window toward the central hall. Ghost or human intruder, I wasn't about to stick around and find out.

I rushed through overhanging tree branches and long grass. I waited until I was far enough away from the house to flick on the flashlight. I stopped in a clearing to catch my breath and think.

CRACK.

Who or what found me? I fumbled to switch off the flashlight and waited in silence. Something was storming through the trees, rapidly gaining on my position.

Fear took hold of me. I fired into the darkness toward the trees, flicking the rifle bolt and chambering another round.

I waited in silence, ears ringing. Did I hit it? I wondered. A piece of me didn't really want to find out, so I turned and headed out of the trees. I stuck to the outskirts of the treeline, staying in the ditch between the dense vegetation and the raised road. My destination was an old horse trail that would eventually lead me to the highway to the nearest town. Taking a breather, I scanned the horizon. Lamppost illuminations flickered in the distance of the reserve's eastern flats, revealing how far the nearest neighbouring homesteads were from me. Even knowing the route, there were many hidden prairie gorges and streams scattered throughout the land. Not to mention badger and coyote dens.

I finally reached the horse trail. I flicked the flashlight back on. The ray sputtered before finally staying on, weaker than it should have been, even if the batteries had been old.

The final grouping of trees cleared and there was nothing but moonlit silhouettes of foothills in front of me. I took one last look over my shoulder and rushed ahead. The flashlight beam glinted off something metallic ahead of me in the tall grass just beside the trail. I cautiously approached. It was my car. How the hell had my Nissan got out here? I moved closer. Shining the flashlight over the car, I saw movement inside. I nearly dropped the rifle and flashlight in surprise. My two beloved dogs were shut inside the car. I tried the door and found it unlocked.

Out jumped Shep, followed by Goose. "What the hell are you two doing in there?" I asked. They jumped in circles, yipping and howling in excitement.

What had I shot at out in the trees? "Come on, you two, let's go," I shouted as I hurried back down the trail toward the ranch.

Cautiously, I skulked up the empty gravel driveway. The front door was wide open. "Who's in here?" I yelled out. "I have a rifle, and I ain't afraid to use it."

Most of the sick jokes that Damien used to play on me and the rest of the younger cousins went too far. Many of them ended up with us being badly hurt.

No answer, but I heard a faint whimper from the living room. I tiptoed through the kitchen and stopped just short of rounding the corner, keeping the rifle at my shoulder.

"Please, don't shoot." It sounded like Damien but strangely choked up, like he'd been crying.

I rounded the corner to find Damien sitting by himself, his head in his hands. "What the hell is going on?" I demanded.

Damien spoke without looking up. "It's all my fault. I'm so sorry, cousin."

"What's all your fault?"

"I swear I didn't mean for it to happen. I just wanted to play a little prank on you. Like old times."

Most of the sick jokes that Damien used to play on

me and the rest of the younger cousins went too far. Many of them ended up with us being badly hurt. "Okay, I'm way lost here. What the hell happened? You have to explain to me right now."

Damien slowly lifted his head, his eyes swimming in tears and his face wet with sorrow. "She's outside," he said.

"Who's outside?"

Damien dropped his face back into his hands.

My heart dropped to the pit of my stomach.

"Damien, who is outside?"

"I'm sorry, cousin," he sobbed.

I bolted down the hall, leaping over the raggedy stairs. My feet were pounding the ground, and tree branches were scrabbling at me as if they were trying to stop me.

I saw the faint glow of a cell phone light ahead. It was lying on the ground in the clearing. Dani was there, kneeling and holding an unmoving body, blood oozing from the chest.

"Brea," I whimpered, dropping my rifle and taking a step forward.

The cellphone light danced off Dani's contorted face. "She's dead."

Damien must have followed me. "I'm so sorry, Axel. I was the one who pressured her into doing it when I ran into her in town. We just wanted to have a little fun with you."

I had once read that a blackout is when the hippocampus fails to process information to the brain's hard drive. In other words: message not sent. I came to with Damien lying in a heap on the ground, his blood looking like black ooze. I looked at the rifle tightly clasped in my hands. The dying, duct-taped flashlight illuminated a small wisp of smoke curling out from the tip of the barrel. My eyes flashed toward Dani. She sat there, but her eyes darted from her dying boyfriend back to the smoking rifle tip.

"What the hell did you do?" she screamed. I stared at her, staying silent as I lay the rifle down at my feet.

SHAWN TEGAN SAT UNMOVING, his face stern.

"Well. Do you think I'm crazy?" Axel asked.

"So ... you, uh, just shot him—your cousin Damien—in cold blood?" Tegan asked.

"Yes. But I also shot my girlfriend. That one was purely accidental, though. I thought she was—well, I just thought she was something inhuman."

"So let me get this straight," said Tegan. "Let's see if I'm on the ball here. Did Damien do something to you as a child? Was that why you shot him?"

"He did. Numerous times. Have you ever heard of some people going through such awful episodes in their lives that they somehow block out that memory—kinda like a blackout?"

"Yes," said Tegan.

"It wasn't until that exact moment when Damien came out of nowhere, right after I found what I'd done to Brea, that I remembered what Damien had done to me."

Tegan leaned back in his chair.

Axel leaned inward. "It was what Damien had done to me as a child. That's what drove me to blackout and pull the trigger on him. So am I still looking at murder?"

Tegan straightened up and fixed his light shimmering tie. "You know what, Mr. Plume? I think we may just have ourselves a fighting chance."

SIX

ACROSS THE
BRIDGE

THE DOWNTOWN CORE of the city is much too lively
for a Sunday night; the honks and squeals of
automobile brakes echo off buildings as if it was rush
hour. I step to the banister. The tempered glass holding it in place is so clear that the thin railing looks like
a free-hanging stretch of wire with nothing below.
Gazing downward, the cars inch through the streets
like fire ants in perfect marching order. I take a final
inhale of my cigarette, hold it in for an extra second,
then exhale, watching the smoke evaporate into the
breezy evening air lit up by the array of sparkling, sky-
scraper illumination. One last look at the horizon illuminated by skyscrapers, and I flick the cigarette butt,
still lit, and keep my eyes trained on it as it spirals out of
control and becomes one with the lively activity below.
I could easily get in trouble for doing what I just did,
even evicted, but what does it matter now?

What to wear? For this evening I choose to go
casual. Nothing too fancy, but still, nothing too fla-
vourless. Chestnut brown Timberland boots and a
knit sweater that reminds me of the old-timer sailors

and fishermen. Classic style. Why not? It isn't summer anymore. "Indian summer" ended a few days ago, and autumn hasn't quite moved in. For my bottoms, blue jeans are the way to go, as it's always been my go-to style, along with a thick, black pea coat, something else that fits in with the nifty knitted sweater.

I wish I could have had more time to say goodbye to my Anubis. She's been the only "lady" in my life for the last four years, and a damn good lady at that. I left her in the care of my friend, Toby, a good person whom I trust will let Anubis live out her remaining days with the comforts I provided for her. The last look she gave me before I closed his apartment door was heartbreaking enough. She already knew. She could probably smell it like the fear that our canine friends sense.

I boot the steel door open and burst out into the street. I'm greeted by the spicy aromas of Dynasty's Chinese Food and smoggy air.

I gave a final once-over of my high-rise condo. Laminate blends well with the rustic, crimson-painted walls, granite kitchen countertops, and furniture straight from the city's warehouse district. Before I leave, do I leave any lights on? Sure, why not? I tug the cord to the lamp my sister bought me as a housewarming gift. I love the thing. It's second-hand, but it would have easily cost an arm and a leg brand new. She's got good taste, my sister.

The dim, solo radiance is not enough. The condo's main sitting area still seems too gloomy. The stove top light fixture hums to life when I flick the switch, the fluorescent bulb sputtering a few times before finally staying lit, spraying the kitchen in a flickering white glow. My shadow casts eerily across the living room floor.

Goodbye, my old domicile. You have provided me well with what I needed in the past few years. It's just too bad I've never had anyone to share it with.

I step out of my unit into the hall that still reeks of fresh paint. So fresh that when I skate the tip of my finger across it, the gummy residue streaks across my trimmed fingernails.

I leave my door unlocked—on purpose and for good reason—and tread down the soft, carpeted hall, the intricate design looking like something straight out of an expensive Turkish hotel. It seems like the walk from my unit to the elevators is at least half a mile long; After uninterrupted, monotonous strolling, I decide I'd rather just take the stairs than wait for one of the elevators to reach my 28th storey stop.

The stairs are long and boring. The chipped grey paint reminds me of abandoned hallways in horror movies. Paired with the eerie echoes of my slow steps down the cold, dusty concrete, a shiver races up my spine.

At last, I reach ground level, where the final-stretch corridor leading to the street is weakly lit by a lone, flickering lamp. It smells of old-man piss. I boot the steel door open and burst out into the street. I'm greeted by the spicy aromas of Dynasty's Chinese Food and smoggy air. The always-open takeout restaurant is well lit, with a steady stream of customers waiting, some already at tables chowing down. Normally, I'd stop in, but not this time. Not tonight.

I walk beneath the underpass, coming out the other side in front of a blinking neon sign that reads: 24/7 Liquors. I walk in like I had been doing every weekend—and some weekdays—for the last, I don't know, I'll just say three years.

"Good evening, Andy," says the beautiful woman behind the till named Kali. Kali comes from India, and I believe her parents named her after the Hindu goddess.

I had once stumbled inside the liquor store just moments before closing, having lost count of how many beers and tequila shots I had slammed back at my favourite watering hole. But whatever the amount I had consumed, I felt like I was a gift from God. In my obliterated state, fresh off a rejection from another beautiful girl in the bar, I had asked Kali out. She said no. Rejected twice in a row, both mere minutes apart.

"Hi," I say monotonously, then walk fast over to the mickey-sized bottles. I grab my good friend Jack Daniels and head casually back to the front of the store, where Kali is looking at me, a slight grin forming on her beautiful lips.

"Hello Andy, how you are doing tonight?" Her sparkling eyes make me think of honey. Usually, at that point I would be melting within, curling my toes on the inside of my shoes in my attempt to suppress any of the affectionate emotions stirring up through my body. Not this time. I keep a stoic façade, like a warrior about to embark upon a war party from which he would not be returning.

"Hey," I say, barely batting an eye. "I'm alright." I say no more and wait, letting her punch the Jack Daniel's purchase amount into the till. She never has to recite the actual price anymore, as it is stamped into my head by now. I hand her a twenty and exit the store before she can protest my leaving her with five dollars in change.

The doorbell chimes and swings slowly shut behind me. I swear I hear her say something like, *Andy, are you okay?* Maybe I heard her, maybe I didn't. Letting go of the thought, I carry on down the mostly empty sidewalk, headlights lighting my path for a few seconds until they cruise by and are out of my life forever.

My destination is near the inner city, the opposite end of the city from where I live, where I once watched a couple of dudes in wetsuits surfing in one spot on the mighty river—the infinite currents of bubbling breakers slamming and criss-crossing over one another like the ocean tsunamis.

THE TRANSIT LINE is only a few minutes' walk, but I decide to take the path less travelled, using the lattices of empty alleys snaking between sprawling skyscrapers. I don't want to see people right now. Or ever again for that matter.

I welcome the darkness, with the only illumination in sight being at the far ends of the alleys, like a single car inside a lonely mountain tunnel. I'm at ease with the relative silence. I can just make out the laughter of people standing on their balconies far above my head, oblivious to me sauntering below in the urine-smelling, unlit alleyway. I walk a few more paces until I see a hollow in the brick wall.

It will have to do.

I slip into the nearly pitch-black doorway and crack open the mickey of Jack Daniels, taking a whiff and letting the potent aroma tingle in my nose. I take a few shots. No chaser. One after another. I drink, until that sickly, warm feeling sloshes around in the pit of my stomach and the 80-proof alcohol feels like anesthetic thickening my tongue.

Not enough. I need to be more intoxicated for my final mission. But I don't want to be too drunk while I'm riding the train. I don't want to make an ass out of myself like I've done so many times. I probably looked like one of the perma-drunks who live their lives panhandling and pestering the commuters aboard the city's transit system.

But first, just one last shot. Save the rest for when I arrive at my final destination.

As I exit the alley, the bright, LED lamps light the rest of my way. I damn near have to shield my eyes as if the sun was at full tilt until I reach the train platform, where I'm bombarded by more blinding LED glare. The clacking of the approaching train rumbles beneath my feet. It is almost empty. I don't take a seat. I choose instead to stand near the sliding doors and use the sturdy perpendicular bar as my crutch as the train lurches forward. The sudden jolt nearly makes my drunken-self stumble to the dirty floor.

While I watch the world of pedestrians and closed shops blur by the large rectangular window, my mind begins to wander. I start to feel sorry for myself, thinking of my latest rejection. Fuel for the mission. Her name is Corina. Beautiful Corina, an Anishinaabe woman from out east. My first day in class was when I spotted her, strolling in late to our student orientation, smiling flawlessly. She had a long, Coke-bottle-shaped body. I swear she was smiling back at me. I mustered up the courage to approach her, asking her to help with a complex math problem I already knew the answer to. That ultimate hello eventually turned to friendship. Friendship turned to Facebook—cyber friendship. Facebook turned to acquiring her cell number. After some months I decided to ask her if she would like to hang out sometime. She said yes, but that *yes* never happened. Every time I asked her to chill, she gave me a different excuse. Eventually, I left well enough alone. No more texts. No more Facebook messaging. No more friendzone excuses.

Corina left me with self-esteem at an all-time low. It took only a few short weeks of self-deliberation to finally come to the series finale I had in mind. Am I not handsome? I've often been told that I was. But it just seems that women who I'm interested in are never interested in me. Enough is enough. Sometimes you just have to know when it's time to call it quits.

My terminus lies just across the river. The paid-fare zone. I forgot to buy a ticket in my half-plastered state of mind as I entered the train. Seldom do transit police ever board this train line, knowing it's away from the inner-city ghetto parts of town. Just my luck, two uniformed transit cops board the train at the last, free-fare zone stop.

My blood turns to ice.

On any other given night, I wouldn't give two shits about not paying the fare, but this time is different. How the hell am I supposed to explain the snub nose .38 snuggled in my breast pocket to two transit peace officers? And that it's meant for me and only me?

My sweat runs like cold, prickly sludge as one of the officers begins hollering to the small crowd of passengers, "Ladies and gentlemen, please have your proof of payment ready in hand. Thank you." He and his partner do a stern once-over of the array of people and begin strolling slowly through the aisle. Cop #1 locks onto my eyes for a split second. He averts his attention elsewhere, then slams his eyes back on me.

He's well-trained in finding the bad guy amongst the good. He walks my way, his eyes locked on me like he's a lion and I'm a lone zebra.

"Hey, partner," says cop #2 to #1, the one eyeing me.

Peeling his eyes off me, #1 swivels to his partner, who has happened upon a passed-out drunk—most certainly also not having paid his transit fare. The lawmen both stand tall over the man and use stern voices to rouse him. No dice. One of the officers then moves on to firm taps, while the other positions himself, ready for the drunk to lunge at him, placing one hand firmly on his holstered canister of pepper spray, the other on a set of shiny steel handcuffs.

"Mister. Wake up. Mister!" says #2 as he prods the prone passenger, his voice loud enough to shatter the large glass window.

The drunken man stirs and grunts. The other passengers, including me, gawk at the spectacle.

Come on, keep your attention focused on him. At least until the end of my short journey—which is literally like thirty seconds away, I plead in silence.

My unsanctioned prayer is answered.

The electronic bell tolls out, and the intercom robot announces my stop. At once I am at the door, throwing a quick glance over my still-shaking shoulder to see the transit cops hard at it with the now-woken man.

Of course, he's Indian, just like me.

DARKNESS ENVELOPS ME as I exit the train station and make my way down the street parallel to the tracks. Just another few minutes and I will be where I'm going. The mighty Bow River. I figure if anyone is peeping out of the many windows from houses lining the streets, it's too dark to see me strolling by. I break out the mickey again and down it until there is nothing left but a venomous drizzle.

Illustration: Alex Soop

Should I say a prayer or something?
Even if I did, what would it do for me?

At last, I arrive at my intended destination. Suddenly I feel cold. A mixture of yellow, white, and other synthetic city colour illuminations dance and sway across the ripples of the rapidly flowing river. I climb the steep, rocky bank, breathe in a heavy gasp, wishing I had bought a pack of cigarettes, and exhale until my lungs feel like they're about to collapse in on themselves. I would kill for a cigarette. I stare hard into the dark. The water teems in a thousand shades of black and blue. I shiver.

It's time.

With shaking hands, I wrestle the zipper on my chest pocket open, reach in, and close my fingers around the pocket-sized pistol. A hell of a fine buy from the man who sells me cocaine by the eight ball. I want my ending to be as painless and effortless as possible, and I've only

129

ever heard that one shot straight through the core of the brain is enough to end it all in a microsecond.

Pain-free.

Lights out.

Well, this is it, I say to myself, eyeing the pistol's silver coating that reflects the downtown sparkle just like the river simmering before my face. Should I say a prayer or something? Even if I did, what would it do for me? Suicide is strictly taboo in the beliefs of the Good Book. But I gave up my Catholic upbringing many years ago, my own opinion lying in the fact that I was living a devout life sanctioned by a religion concocted by the same people who crucified their own savior and, above all else, the ones who tried their absolute best to destroy my People's way of life.

"Goodbye," I whisper. I cock the pistol's hammer.

"Hi. Whatcha doin' over there?"

The sudden southern drawl of a voice is enough to make me stumble back, nearly losing footing on the rocky boulders. I grapple with the pistol, which bounces around in my juggling hands before it goes spiralling from my grip, landing with a disheartening sploosh in the seething blackness below.

"Dammit," I scream out, furiously twisting to face the person who just interrupted my final mission. "You stupid son of a—" My words fall dead.

She is beautiful. Out of my league, beautiful.

I stare without making a sound, holding my breath so that my vision has a chance to smooth out over the wobbly shudders of my galloping heart.

I try to look away but can't. There's nothing else worth looking at. Her hair is a shimmering scarlet, twirling past her shoulders with black tips that look like burnt ends on a matchstick. She isn't dressed for the crisp fall weather, instead she wears leggings beneath a long sleeve cotton T-shirt with white perforated lace, the sleeves rolled up to her forearms.

"You jus' drop somethin'?" she asks.

"Yeah." I reply. "I dropped my uhh—cellphone." I lied. I had factory reset my latest model smartphone just a few hours prior and left it on a bus stop bench for some lucky passerby to stumble across.

"From where I stand, was kinda a funny lookin' phone to me. But is there anything I can do, you know, to help get it back for ya?" she asks.

I glance down at the roiling water. "No, it's—it's gone. Long gone by now. Even so, the water damage would be beyond repair." I face her again.

"Oh no darlin', I'm real sorry about that. If I had a phone on me, I would happily offer it to ya. But I just got here you see; I'm wearin' everything I own." She does a quick twirl on the lone boulder she stands upon, revealing a small pack belted to her back by thin, leathery straps.

There's no way this beauty is homeless. She even smells like roses—not a smell you encounter with the domestically challenged.

"Where are you from?" I ask, the only question that comes to mind.

"Far from here. Where the trees are green all year round, the flowers are always in bloom, and the water flows without ever seein' a sliver of frost or ice," she says, a smile forming to reveal teeth white enough to blaze through the darkness.

"Texas. No, East Texas? Or how about N'Orleans?"

She giggles and covers her mouth politely. "You're cute. Close enough, I'll jus' say to that. Now, you ain't upset about your cellphone I done made you drop into that cold, cold' water?"

I look at the raging water again. "No, it's all good. I was thinking of selling the piece of crap anyways."

"Alright. Well, my name is Angela. But you can go 'head and call me Angie if that works better for ya." She steps off her rock and extends her hand up to me from the grassy bank, her milky white skin glowing.

I'm just gonna come out and say it: You are the
last person I ever expected to stumble across.
Someone as beautiful as you, and
especially on a cold and lonely night like this.

I finally step down from my massive boulder pedestal. "Here, take my jacket." I place the heavy wool coat around her slender frame. "My name is Andrew. But you can go ahead and call me Andy if you like."

"Andy or Andrew?" she says with a charming giggle, tightening the coat around her petite frame. She takes a step closer. "I prefer Andrew if it's all the same to you. It jus' sounds much more important."

I snicker. "Alrighty then. Now that we got that outta the way. Would you care to take a stroll with me? The mist from this water is making me shiver." Another lie, but she doesn't need to know how nervous I am.

"Y'can have your jacket back if ya like. I don't really—"

"No, no, you hold onto it. What kind of gentleman would I be if I just let you go cold? And besides, this sweater keeps me pretty cozy. Listen, could you eat? I know I sure can go for a bite right about now," I say, hoping that she accepts my offer to just go somewhere and sit with her.

"Actually, darlin', I already had me a bite to eat not long ago. But I will most definitely be delighted to join ya if that's alright?" She takes a step back and sticks out her arm creased into a hook and awaits with another heart-warming smile.

I take in her invitation, snake my arm through hers, lock it at the elbow, and guide her up the grassy bank until we reach the paved pathway. "What a helluva thing," I say bluntly, speaking the exact words on my mind.

"Come again?"

"I'm just gonna come out and say it: You are the last person I ever expected to stumble across. Someone as beautiful as you, and especially on a cold and lonely night like this."

"Why, thank you, you're so sweet. And to be honest, I kinda like this weather. It's a change from the usual heat that I'm accustomed to back home." She speaks with an elegant style in her southern belle accent.

"I haven't been the luckiest dude lately—for quite some time actually. And that's the doggone truth."

"Well, it seems we may have a lengthy walk ahead of us." She pulls herself in tighter to me, nearly leaning her head on my shoulder like we were a close-knit couple. "Care to indulge me?"

WE WALK FOR HOURS on end through the pathways lining the downtown outskirts as I pour my heart out to this girl I've just met, including my many relationship misfortunes. She is a good listener. I feel like I'm in a dream, and I never want to wake up. I've even almost overlooked the fact that I had come within seconds of taking my own life had she not interrupted.

Lucky for me.

The narrow bike and pedestrian trail we are promenading winds through an open park bordering the river's edge, ultimately splitting off into a Y, the branch of the trail crossing the river by way of the pedestrian bridge.

"Well, I know I can definitely eat right about now... where were you planning on staying tonight?" I ask.

Angela, as I decide to call her since it sounds more important than Angie, slows her pace a bit, lost in thought. She stares hard through the darkness surrounding us for a moment before finally looking at me with her sparkling eyes. "Well, I wasn't too sure about that. I was thinkin' maybe one of them hostels that cost next to nothin."

"No way," I blurt. "Haven't you heard on the news what happens to pretty, unaccompanied girls like you that stay at those places? Stay at my condo tonight. I have a super comfortable bed and—"

She slams the brakes on our walk and throws me a lopsided glare, her smile twisting into a scowl.

"As I was saying, my bed is super comfortable. And so is my couch; so therefore, I don't mind at all letting you sleep on my bed—while I sleep on the couch, of course."

She squeezes my arm tightly and we begin casually walking again. "You surely are a gentleman, y'know that, Mr. Andrew? I would be delighted to sleep on your bed—with you right next to me, of course," she says with a wink, planting a wet kiss on my wind-bitten cheek. "Can I jus' ask one thing?" she says, once again applying the brake pedal to our stroll.

"Yes. By all means."

"Was that a gun you were holding back there before I gone and startled you down by the river?"

I can't lie to the woman who literally just saved my life. "Yeah. Yeah, it was," I answer dolefully, hoping she doesn't relinquish her embrace and storm off in fear.

"Well then, it's more than good that I made you drop it into the river," she says sweetly.

"I would say so. That's for damn sure."

"Mmmm, okay," she leans her head against my shoulder, and we begin walking again, saying nothing in our newfound moment of comfortable silence.

SEX IS ON MY MIND. It's the nature of man. Or at least, it's the nature of this man. I may or may not get it, but that's more than okay because, for the moment, I'm simply pleased to be in the company of a soft-hearted, beautiful woman who sees me for the real me. I smile with gratitude and look ahead of us. The pedestrian bridge is lit up brilliantly in a cluster of rainbow hues, with LED lights glistening like a kaleidoscope. "Come on, let's hurry up. I want to show you this bridge the city just installed."

She responds with a smile and picks up her step in unison with mine.

As we cross the bright rainbow-showered bridge, I am once again mesmerized. I see her much more clearly, as though it was the middle of the day, maybe even better from the brilliant hues of the bright, oscillating lights. For some reason, I'm reminded of candy. Her hair is like strands of flawless Twizzler licorice, gentle waves and single strands of flowing red rivers, and her skin is smooth white chocolate. Her eyes are dark like black coals, drawing me in. Everything about her is perfect, her high cheekbones to match my own. Everything.

"Well. Are you just gonna stand there and gawk, or are we gonna go somewhere nice and warm?" she asks playfully.

I snap myself out of my trance and mumble, "Um, yeah—no. Let's, um, let's head back to my place. I can always heat something up. And maybe you might be hungry by then."

She giggles. "Yeah, maybe."

I can tell she isn't from a big city; she stares at the polished steel of the entrance door handles like it's pure gold from some Pharaoh's tomb.

"If that excites you, just wait until you see the interior. Come on." I use my keychain fob to bypass the door's automated security lock and hold the door open for her. She smiles with a curtsy and steps through, hunching over to admire the silvery trim of the vestibule housing. "No, that's not it either." I laugh, open the secondary door, and wave her in.

She nods at the doorman security posted behind his desk. "May I?" she asks, pointing to the inner alcove of the lobby decorated to look like a dream of distant rainforests.

"Yeah, you go on. I'll be with you in a minute." I stop to check my mailbox, not caring that it was past midnight on a Monday morning. Routine habit. Nothing inside but junk mail, of course. I saunter past the security desk, nodding at Stephen, the guard's name—one of my only friends in the building. "Hey there Steve-O," I say. He slowly nods at me with wide, disbelieving eyes. He never was big on words. I walk a little taller through the lobby until I catch up with Angela, her petite hands rubbing at the overhanging leaf of one of the simulated palm trees.

"It's fake," she says.

"Of course, it is," I reply. "It's cold here for most of the year, so it's pretty hard to keep real ones alive. Let's head upstairs. It's a twenty-eight-storey elevator ride."

Her dark eyes flash in the bright lobby. "Lead the way, darlin."

"This is it," I tell her as we approach the last door at the end of the hall. I haven't had a girl in my condo in well over two years, and even that went horribly wrong, my date got intoxicated and nearly fell from my balcony. My nerves still tighten at the recollection of that near miss of a night.

"I can't wait," Angela says excitedly.

My door that I had left unlocked swings open and bangs into the doorstop, making me startle, as it does every time. At least I left the light on, my sister's house-warming gift. "Well, this here is the coat closet. I'll just take—" Angela bypasses my outstretched hand, still wearing my jacket that's a few sizes too big on her and walks straight down the short corridor. I watch her until she vanishes around the corner. "Right behind ya," I whisper to myself.

I turn the corner and see her standing almost motionless in the centre of the living room, staring at the big screen TV, then the kitchenette island bar top with four silver-trimmed stools tucked neatly underneath.

"This apartment, it's jus' so nice," she says.

Condo, I correct in my mind. "So, you like?"

"I love," she says and turns to face me, radiating the slightest colour. But still pallid. Fresh-snow pallid.

"Well, I'm glad to hear that. Would you care to see the view of downtown from twenty-eight storeys up?" *A real panty dropper,* a buddy had once said about this view.

"Would I ever."

I slide open the heavy glass door, step out onto the

balcony, take her hand in mine, and slowly lead her out beside me. She clutches my fingers tightly as she leans into me against the silver banister. She admires the sparkling city lights for a few moments before turning to face me. I lean her back against the rail, and she draws me in until I can feel her sweet breath on my lips.

We stare wordlessly into each other's eyes until I break the silence by whispering, "So, you gonna tell me where you're from, or do I have to keep on guessing until I get it right?"

She says nothing, a smile dimpling the corners of her mouth, and places her cool finger to my warm lips. "Come," she finally says and draws me into a dizzying kiss.

I DIDN'T RECEIVE THE SEX that I had high hopes for, but still, that's more than okay with me. I wake up, the lamp on my nightstand still powered on with its warm radiance causing my sitting shadow to dance happily on the opposite wall. Angela is sleeping, her delicate features unmoving. My mind is awash with memories of last night. *"You are such a beautiful and gentle loving man. Any woman would be lucky to have you in her life,"* she said to me just before nestling against my chest and closing her eyes.

I tread quietly to the kitchen for a drink of water and return to my bedroom, feeling the after-effects of the whiskey beginning to hit me. Angela is still curled up in my bed. I slip under the sheets and join her, draping my arm over her gently so as not to awaken her. Sleep comes fast and easy with her by my side.

ALL I HEAR is her perfect voice speak my name and utter something else in the haziest of whispers in my ear before I feel her cool lips kiss my cheek.

Was it a dream?

I wake with the stout tang of stale whiskey thick on the roof of my mouth. The coppery taste is enough to overpower the sense of flabbergast churning through my hungover head. I turn to my side to steal an early morning glance at Angela.

Her side of the bed is empty.

"Angela," I call out, hoping to see her rush into my room wearing one of my baggy T-shirts. "Angie?"

Nothing.

I roll off my bed and amble into the living room, the sides of my head thumping like a ceremonial drum. My pulse quickens. So does the drum. The living room and kitchenette are empty, the sliding glass door to the patio still wide open.

Someone knocks at the door.

Ahh, she probably just went down to the store to grab us a bite to eat. I rush to the door and wrench it open.

"Uhh, hey there, Andy," says Stephen, the security doorman. He looks concerned.

"Good morning," I say and crane my neck to take a look down the hall. Still no Angela in sight.

"Hey uhh," Stephen begins. "Look, I dunno how to say it. So, I'm a just come straight out. You okay, man? Like, really okay?"

I lean back and feel my eyebrows shoot up my forehead. "Yeah. I'm good. Never better. Why do you ask, old friend?"

"Had a little to drink last night?"

"You were able to tell, were ya?"

He relaxes. "I can smell the aftermath as we speak. Remember, I gave up the ol' bottle going on thirteen years now."

"Yeah, I admit it. I had me a bit to drink last night. But Stephen ol' buddy, if you don't mind, I have a lot on my plate right now. You know I'd usually be down to chat it up with you, but I'm actually waiting on someone," I say, sounding as self-possessed as possible.

"Yeah," he says again, scratching at something just above his ear, "about that—"

"What?" I'm getting a little testy. Could be the drums banging against my skull; could be I still haven't found Angela.

The late morning sun is high in the sky, its rays bouncing off nearby glass buildings and spraying the streets in its warmth.

"Look. Reason I'm up here checking on you—and you know as well as anyone that is *not* part of my job description—is that you came in last night, and you were... uhh... well, you were talking to yourself."

"What?" I feel a weird laugh bubbling up in my throat.

"Yeah. You remember seeing me, right?"

"Of course, I do. But I wasn't talking to myself. I was talking to the girl that came in with me. You didn't see her?"

Stephen sighs heavily. "Would you care to come down to the security office? I'd rather show you than tell you. Know what I mean?"

"What, you have some men in white coats waiting downstairs or something?" I tease.

He just stares at me, then shakes his head.

"Alright," I exhale, puffing out my cheeks. "Let me just grab a coat." I turn and head back into the bedroom, quickly write a note for Angela, find a sweatshirt from the closet, and join Stephen for the short trek down to his security office.

I NEED TO CLEAR MY HEAD. The thrashing hangover does nothing to help my panic. I burst out of Stephen's security office, whiskey sweat oozing from every pore, ignoring Stephen's attempts to comfort me. I shrug off his brotherly touch from my shoulder.

A drink. What I need right now is a stiff drink.

Had I really been talking to myself? The proof was all there. All high definition, 1080 pixels of it. I held the door open for no one, even waved that no one in, then strolled past Stephen's security desk, grinning like a fool. I nodded my head at Stephen, but not before stopping to face the empty hall, speaking to nobody before checking my empty mailbox. No one at all. Stephen said that I also went down the hall and stopped at one of the palm trees—and yet again carried on a one-sided conversation with air.

The weather outside has turned cooler. The late morning sun is high in the sky, its rays bouncing off nearby glass buildings and spraying the streets in its warmth. Sun means people, and there are lots of them, most paying me no attention. Good.

I speed walk, slowing my pace as I enter the underpass, a loud, slow-moving train on the tracks directly above. The cool air is refreshing, calming my throbbing head just a bit. Two more minutes. I pick up my pace again and finish walking through the shade until the sun once more warms my face.

A homeless man sleeping on the sidewalk outside 24/7 Liquors bugs me for change, so I fish in my pockets and hand over whatever I have. Six dollars and fifty-five cents.

"Thanks," he says as I step over his outstretched legs, his old work boots caked in dust and grime.

I reach for the flat door handle and halt with only a bit of hesitation. I remember what the beautiful redheaded apparition had said to me. "Maybe you shouldn't drink so much if you're feelin' sad. Alcohol only makes it worse. I would know, darlin'." Angela's southern belle words drift through my otherwise heavy thoughts. But if she hadn't been there, then who or what said those things? It couldn't have been my conscience; that's what told me to buy the pistol and end my life.

But was it my conscience?

Food. My stomach growls.

I take a quick detour to the always-open curry and pizza joint located in the same strip mall as 24/7 Liquors. The air is just right inside, and I order the usual and take my customary seat, my mind occupied with intense images of Angela.

There's no way she could have been just a figment of my imagination. She was too real. Too peculiar for me to concoct.

"Mister Andrew," interrupts Assad, the restaurant's owner. I turn to face his gracious smile. "Your food is ready, my friend." He smiles, places the butter chicken and rice on my table, and walks away.

Well, I guess I better eat, I think. *And then maybe I should grab a soda pop over a mickey.* I begin chowing down on the tantalizing food when I feel a light tap on my shoulder. I swallow before turning to face whoever it is.

It's a good thing I swallowed my food because my mouth drops open in wonder of who it is standing before me. Here she is in person, carting a charming smile that is the most beautiful fixation I have been fortunate enough to lay eyes on, her honey-coloured eyes glittering like heaven-sent stars in the brilliance of the bright sun.

"Hi. May I join you?" asks Kali. As I jump to my feet to pull back a chair for her, it occurs to me that my loyal canine friend Anubis might also make her way back into my life. I will see if Kali wants to come over to Toby's with me to pick her up.

～ SEVEN ～

MR. KNIFE

I SPENT TWO YEARS IN PRISON. Drumheller Penitentiary, or just plain old 'Drum' as people who do time there call it. I served two years of a five-year sentence. It's true what they say—good behaviour really does get you a head start on early release. Parole. Even then, the government still owns your ass until your warrant expiry.

Minus a few traffic tickets, I was a pretty law-abiding citizen. My sports car got me in the only trouble with the law before my prison stint. More serious this time was the charge pitted against me of 'Aggravated Assault with a Weapon.'

Prison was definitely not a place for a guy like me— an introvert—not a loner or a shut-in. I much prefer the company of a few trustworthy friends or family, my girl, or a loyal dog for that matter over a bunch of criminally minded fellas on any given day.

Prior to prison, I had been dating a beautiful girl for about eight months. I met her while shopping at a local supermarket. She looked lost. She was too short to reach a box of cereal on the top shelf. This was my call to approach her, and I'm glad I did.

She was younger than me, twenty-one to my twenty-eight. I was damn near out of what were supposed to be the best years of my life, and she was just starting hers. So naturally, I felt lucky that she chose to be with me. Unlike past relationships she had been in, I never hit her. I never will.

Despite being just over five-feet tall, Mia had a vibrant gymnast's body with shapely long legs for her size. Her light brown hair with tints of blonde was always cut short; she kept it cropped just above her shoulders, and it danced when she moved.

And Mia's eyes—oh, those eyes—her absolute best feature: slightly narrow, sharp, and alluring. They drew you in like they had their own gravitational pull. Depending on her mood, they also morphed colours, from brown to hazel to a light greyish green. She was light-skinned like me, maybe a few shades darker. Absolutely gorgeous. She hailed from way up in northern Alberta, the land of ceaseless scrubland and lush evergreen forests. She was of Dene descent.

I am from the deep southern plains of Alberta. Blackfoot. Nitsiitapi.

My home reserve, the Blood Tribe, a name given to us by the Canadian government, is one of the largest in land size in North America. Where I grew up, at the very southwest end of the reserve, is a place called Bullhorn. Bullhorn is a place of beauty. It's where the sea of gold and olive drab grasslands sway and ripple in the ever-present wind, which washes down from the snow-capped peaks of the Rocky Mountains.

Just beyond the initial peaks of the Rockies in a plateau surrounded by emerald-blue lakes lies a small tourist town called Waterton. It's a perfect little spot to take your lover, especially in the dead middle of the high, midsummer heat. Mia had never been out west to the neighbouring province of British Columbia, nor had she ever been to the Rockies, for that matter. Mia, who I was gung-ho crazy about, was about to embark on a personalized scenic tour of southern Alberta, guided by me. It was my very own backyard, after all.

It was an unusually warm long weekend in May, May Long as we call it, giving a taste of the scorching summer to come. The car ride was pleasant. We had the sunroof open the entire way. It's usually about a three-and-a-half-hour trip from Calgary to Waterton without any stops. We ended up taking four and a half, with more than one stop for spontaneous romance.

The first leg of the journey took us on a relaxing cruise across a large, prairie established highway with panoramic views of beautiful river-lacerated valleys and farmlands, the looming Rockies standing tall in the westerly backdrop. The final segment of the journey lies at the foot of the Rocky Mountains. A narrow two-lane road twists and slices through isolated foothills. The mountains lie so close you could almost throw a stone at them. They've always reminded me of the Mountains of Mordor, from the Lord of the Rings, in the way they materialize in the clouds. Just watching us.

Midway through the desolate two-lane highway, there's a nifty Mexican-style cantina. We pulled into the roadside restaurant and bar for a snack and a break, seating ourselves at a small round table beneath an outdoor awning where the view was breathtaking. The food was good, and they served Corona. I was a little taken aback at the authentic meal; I didn't think there were a lot of Mexican folks in the farthest reaches of southwest Alberta. I slammed back only two of the imported lagers, not wanting to get buzzed—nor to break the law—then we got back on the road.

By that time, the sun was starting to drop behind the Rockies. Being with Mia gave me a renewed insight into how beautiful the skies are from the base of the mountain slopes. The transition between the black-ridged embankments, with their pointed peaks stabbing up at a sky of explosive blue, pink, and gold hues was awe-inspiring.

I was glad to have a low-riding,
road-hugging sports car instead of
some jacked-up truck on that stretch of road.

The brightness of the high-tech headlights I'd just installed skated across the blacktop, and as shadows deepened, the roadside foliage became silhouettes. The enveloping darkness with barely visible twilight glowing above the mountain tops gave me the feeling of being surrounded by colossal monsters. Mia had fallen asleep by this time, and so I felt somewhat alone driving through that shadowy landscape.

The road then narrowed out. It twisted, dipped, and curved sharply through the hilly terrain. I had to slow down to avoid swerving over the sharp edge of the road. I was glad to have a low-riding, road-hugging sports car instead of some jacked-up truck on that stretch of road.

For the rest of our journey through the dark, only one vehicle passed us. It was an old rickety pickup truck from the 1970s, and it couldn't have passed us at a worse time. I had to brake hard and veer onto the gravel shoulder to let it pass us on the winding highway. To my astonishment, the driver never slowed and seemed not the least bit bothered by my blinding headlamps in his rear-view mirror. I switched my beams from dim to bright to express my displeasure to him. No dice. He just kept on moving past us like a maniac.

At last, we came to a junction to the outskirts of Waterton, where fir trees dominated the landscape. I keep saying "we" as though Mia had been awake the entire time. Nope. She was sleeping like a conked-out kid. Maybe she was so full of Mexican food that now was her time to siesta. It was after 11:00 p.m., and I was expecting more road traffic, what with it being a long weekend. Even the small national park admission huts were void of personnel. All of them were already out on the town, I speculated, enjoying the fun.

With nobody to stop me, I carried on ahead through the bypass lane.

The moon was out, its beautiful silvery glow skimming across the tops of the trees and glinting off the placid lakes in the valleys. I had been to Waterton enough times to know that there was a steep embankment just off the shoulder of the highway to my left. Going over the edge would be deadly. If the ridged rocks below didn't kill us, then the icy cold, glacial lake waters surely would. I kept my speed well below the posted limit.

Relief washed over me as I steered by the visitor information centre. Tall LED street lights lit the place up on both sides. At a quick glance I saw a few vehicles parked: two SUVs, a National Parks truck, a fancy sports car, a jacked-up off-road truck, and a minivan with a family of five loading cargo through its large rear door. I wondered if I should pull in to use the men's facility, but I didn't. There would be a gas station in town for that.

At last, the lights of the town came into full bloom. My spirit warmed at the beautiful sights from the height of the winding mountain road and down to the urban glow glimmering across the lake's gently rippling surface. Mia looked beautiful and at peace as she slept, but I really needed to use the bathroom, so I gently nudged Mia awake and informed her we had arrived at our destination.

As she awoke, her eyes lit up and sparkled like fireworks.

I pulled into the nearest gas station and told the attendant to throw in twenty dollars. Mia said she didn't have to pee, but she got out of the car anyway and stared in astonishment at the silhouettes of the Rockies with the moon glowing just above their jagged peaks.

I went inside alone. The store was real touristy: there were rotating metal shelves full of postcards and keepsake memorabilia, artsy wooden shelves displaying glassware and stuffed animals, especially bears and elk, plus toys and snacks. Hats and t-shirts with funky writing on them and an array of cheap sunglasses lined the walls. A teenager manning the till asked if he could help me. I paid for the gas and asked him where the bathrooms were. He gave me the key to the men's room around the back on the outside. I thanked him and followed his instructions.

I came back, purchased a few iced teas, and returned the key. Mia was already outside of the car, standing and watching in awe at the display of the moon, a swathe of clouds skating in between the heavenly glow and the mighty Rocky Mountain peaks. She eyed me with a smile I'll never forget.

"Come on, I wanna show you something cool." I waved her over, and she followed me back to the car.

The heat from earlier in the day rose off the freshly refurbished blacktop, giving the cool mountain air a hint of warmth. We cruised slowly down the small cobblestone main street with the windows rolled down. The town seemed livelier than it had looked from our approach. Shops and restaurants had their front doors wide open. Many of them had music pouring out into the streets. Couples walked about, window shopping. A group of teens were following one another in a flying V formation like geese, chattering cheerfully, each of them holding their smartphones in front of them like scanners. Outdoor patios were full of patrons, wining and dining, while ice cream shops were full of cheerful patrons.

"Everything's still open?" Mia asked me.

"Yup. Until midnight. It's the town's opening day. May long weekend. But only on this one night will they be open this late."

We finally came to the end of the township road and pulled into a small campground leading down to the lakeside beach. An assortment of tents littered the green park flats.

We both cleared out the car.

"We're gonna stay here?" Mia asked cautiously, her eyes drained of the excitement that had lit them up only seconds prior.

I snickered. "No. We don't even have a tent. There's just a lil' something over here I gotta show you. I've been visiting it since I was a kid."

Hand in hand, we walked along the road, alongside

fenceless neighbourhoods with small, paved drive-ways. To our right was a medium-sized school park surrounded by evergreen trees and an assortment of planted trees not native to the region. The areas were well lit by tall street lamps, radiating with an amber glow.

"You hear that?" asked Mia, stooping low like she was listening for something.

"That's what I wanted to show you. It's just over there." I pointed to an area beyond the street lamps' reach, across a small bridge. All we could see from the road was a grouping of fifty-foot-tall evergreens surrounded by darkness.

"Umm, no. It's dark over there, and we don't even have a flashlight. Or do you?" she asked.

"Why? Are you scared?" I was being a bit frisky with her.

"It looks dangerous." Mia's voice wavered as she hugged herself tightly.

"Oh, come on, don't be scared. I'll protect you. Besides, there's no one else out here but us. Might be a few grizzly bears, or maybe a mean old wildcat. Ah hell, there might even be a hungry pack of wolves. But I swear that's about it."

She batted me lightly on the chest. "Ugh, I can't believe you just said that. I'm going back to the car. Give me the keys."

"Wait. Hold on." I stood motionless.

"Did you see something?" she asked, her adorable eyes darting around, trying to see through the darkness.

"There. Better late than never." I pointed ahead of where we stood. The dark, tree-filled area was suddenly brightened by a group of hidden park lamps.

"Oh, wow! I can see it now." She grasped my arm

tight and tugged me toward her as she ran toward the lights.

We crossed the bridge and followed a paved path until we came to the base of a rocky incline. In the corner of the steep, stony bluffs was a magnificent waterfall that stood at least a hundred feet high. The falls churned and splashed frothy white as they crashed with a deafening roar to the ice-cold plunge pool below. We proceeded onto an antique bridge just over the mist billowing from beneath the falls.

"You feel that?" she said, lifting her nose to the night sky and closing her eyes. A cool biting mist swirled around her lamp-lit face.

"I figured you'd like this."

"I do. I love it. Can we get closer?"

"We can. But what about the bears and whatnot?" I joked.

She thought for a moment and shrugged her shoulders. "Meh. Let's just go anyway."

Ducking under a rickety wooden fence barrier, we headed for the end of the grounds and abruptly came up against the rocky embankment, rising up at a ninety-degree angle. The chilly mist from the falls started to soak the outer layer of my jacket.

"Well, this is it," I said, my excitement waning as I began to shiver uncontrollably. "Wanna go back to the lake?"

"Yes," she replied. She also didn't look like she was enjoying the combination of frosty mist and chilly night air.

Following a few moments of admiring the falls, we strolled back the way we had come, arriving back at the small campground. There were tents teeming with campers all around the beachside clearing. From within the colourful nylon structures, kids giggled and joked around. A few of the fire pits had families surrounding them, chatting and roasting hot dogs and marshmallows on dancing flames.

Hands entwined, Mia and I made our way down to the rocky beach and found a small wooden bench and plopped down on it. We ogled at the wonder of the perfectly still lake; not a ripple could be seen on its black, moonlit-mirror surface.

"Can we go for a drink?" she asked, giving my hand a squeeze.

"I'm down for that," I said. "I know a lil' spot. Come on, let's roll."

We walked back into the town site via the main street sidewalk. By then, it was almost midnight, and the bustling activity was now down to a low murmur of only a few people here and there. A few blocks in, and we found the destination I had in mind: The Hungry Bear.

Guarding the front entrance of the bar stood a massive grizzly bear statue in attack mode, claws at the ready. Inside the bar looked like a saloon, with oak bars and furnishings. Oak everything. Even the floor was a sturdy, stained wood covering. The sounds of classic rock drifted through the stale, beery air. An array of neon signs adorned the wooden walls.

The place was pretty dead, except for a few nearby tables of loud and giggling drunken people who looked to be around our own age. I had been in that bar on a few occasions on May long weekends, and I recalled it being packed to the brim. We walked up a small ramp leading off the dance floor and found a nice empty booth to ourselves.

"Hi there. May I take your order?" asked a tall, slim, beautiful woman. She had long wavy black hair that flowed like a river past her shoulders and came to a dead stop on her chest.

I smiled overly politely at her and asked for a moment to look over our menus. She said to wave her over when we were ready.

"What the hell was that?" Mia snapped at me.

"What was what?" I asked, looking up at her over my menu.

"The way you looked and even smiled at her. Couldn't have been more obvious there, bud." She was furious. The only time Mia ever called me bud was when she was upset with me.

"Come on now. Please, don't start this." I said, rolling my eyes. Native women can burst out with realness when situations like this call for a reality check. It's all part of their truth and charm.

"Well, then don't bring me all the way down here just so you can start hitting on the first hot woman you see!" She raised her voice high enough so that the tables across the bar floor had heard her. Each and every one of the patrons were curiously staring at us.

"Really?" I knew Mia had an insecure spot in her heart, but I had never cheated on her.

"I just wanna go home," she said, betraying her bad mood due to weariness.

"What about drinks? Aren't you hungry?"

"Not anymore, I'm not. Get me outta here. Now!" She slammed the top of the table with her open palm. The jolt must've hurt because she let out a loud scream. Loud enough that one of the patrons from a distant table came to investigate.

He was a tall man with broad shoulders and a keg for a belly. Maybe a once-good football player in his prime days, now he was just another case-of-beer slammin' farm boy. "Everything okay over here, folks?" he asked. His face was deep red from an overabundance of time in the sun.

"We're good," I said irritably. "Please leave us be, dude."

"Whoa, there now. No need to get angry with me. I just came to see if the little miss was okay."

I just didn't want to have to fight and end up hurting this big sloppy guy. I'd been coached against getting involved in street fights.

"Little miss?" barked Mia. "Umm, excuse me, who's little here? Your cock?" I had to turn my face away to hide my laughter.

"Now you better just be stoppin' right there," said the man. His face reddened enough that it almost glowed beneath his sweat-blemished white trucker cap. I could tell he was infuriated—or embarrassed. Maybe a little bit of both. "You best check your miss there, buddy."

I shrugged my shoulders. "Can't help you there, man. The girl says what she wants to say. And that's that." I glanced at Mia. She was glowering at him.

"So, you just gonna let the lil' girl fight your battles, huh?" he sneered, his thin moustache quivering as he spoke.

"Battles?" I asked. "No battles here. Hell, you just came along and butted your thick ass nose in our business."

"Now those right there are fightin' words, buddy!"

Before I could react, Mia scrambled out of her side of the booth and cocked her arm as though she was going to swing at the burly intruder. I sprung out of my side of the booth and grabbed her by the forearm, halting her swift momentum in the nick of time. I had no idea until that moment the extent of how jealous and chippy she could be.

The man took a step back. "I'll see you out in the parking lot," he snarled before scampering off like a large dog with its tail tucked between its legs.

My hands were still holding onto Mia's shaking forearm. She wrenched herself free. "Geez, now, look," I said. "I might have to fight this big ol' goof."

Mia wrinkled her nose and grinned.

I had been training in mixed martial arts with my bigger, younger brother for at least three years. I won my only two amateur fight-card matches, both within the first three rounds. I just didn't want to have to fight and end up hurting this big sloppy guy. I'd been coached against getting involved in street fights. As for my imminent contender, I knew about these kinds of guys, having come of age in the countryside.

What if this guy was a dirty fighter who invited his friends to jump in? Or maybe he was a respectable old-school scrapper and would do it fairly one-on-one. Either way, I wasn't in the mood to fight. And besides, both players always ended up walking away with more than just bruises.

I nodded at the guy, and we exited the bar. My plan of action was to talk it out with the guy. You know? Be the better man, as they say.

Mia followed me outside and said, "He's a jerk and I know you want to kick the shit out of him, but let's just get out of here and go back to the city."

"I'm not going to fight, Mia. I'm just gonna talk it out. Like real men," I said in assurance.

The group the man had been drinking with stumbled out of the bar like a spooked herd of cattle.

"Let's do this!" The man shouted. He was strutting around like a champion fighter making a big entrance into the ring.

Solemnly and calmly, I walked over to the man with my open hands half raised in the air, a universal sign of no harm intended.

Then I saw it. It gleamed like an emerald in the bright moonlight. A translucent pearlescent handle stuck out from his brown leather belt. It had not been there in the bar.

Keeping myself composed, I began speaking in a cool, calm manner: "Look, guy. If you're thinking about busting out that—"

Too late.

The coward clutched the buck knife handle in his right hand, hastily unsheathed it from his belt, and swung aggressively in my direction. I bobbed out of the way. I felt a whiff of wind from the blade carving through the air inches from my nose. He must have thrown all his body weight into the slash attempt because he lost his balance. By thrusting down on his shoulder blades with my open palms, I helped him topple over, smack onto the ground.

Just like that, the fight was over.

Or at least it should have been.

Despite knowing that one should never kick a man when he's down, this guy had broken the first and oldest unwritten rule of fistfights: he'd brought a weapon. I sent some kicks to the side of his grounded torso. The man's body shuddered violently, and he cried out as I felt the crunch of breaking ribs.

I ceased my ground-and-pound kicking when I felt Mia's fingers clamp down on the base of my neck. I spun around to face her.

"Stop. Please stop!" she cried, wide-eyed. "Oh, God, you're going to kill him!" Tears streamed down her cheeks.

I dropped my arms to my sides and stood immobile. Breathing heavily and staring down at the man, I backed up a few steps to let his concerned friends see to him. He was in a state of agony.

It seemed like only a few minutes passed before emergency sirens rang out through the still nighttime air. The mountains made the sirens echo, like the bells of calamity tolling me closer to my fate.

I knew I was in trouble.

I DIDN'T THINK FOR ONE INSTANT that I was going to be in as much trouble as I was. After all, it was self-defence, right? Wrong. "Aggravated Assault with a Weapon, and Assault Causing Bodily Harm" were the charges the justice system handed down to me. All the man's friends had been appointed as key witnesses at my trial. Of course, I pleaded not guilty. Even the tall and beautiful server with the wavy black hair agreed to testify against me. It was all their words against Mia's. According to them (probably to protect their bozo of a friend from the strong arm of the law), I initiated the fight by shoving the man to the ground. And, of course, there was no knife. I was the weapon. Having a martial arts background makes you a "dangerous weapon" in the eyes of the law.

I was screwed.

Following a year of house arrest and, ultimately,

my trial procedure, they let me hug my family and Mia after my sentencing. Although a goodbye kiss to Mia was strictly ruled out.

I was off to prison.

A few of the processing sheriffs were aware of my amateur wins in mixed martial arts. They respected and treated me somewhat fairly as they shackled me up and took my civilian shoes and jacket. The shithole remand centre was my place of residence for a week while they found me a bed at old Drumheller Penitentiary. "Strip down. Show us your arse. Spread em!" I was humiliated.

I arrived at Drumheller Penitentiary a week after my sentencing.

I traded in my leather jacket for a dull green, garbage-man-looking coat. Even worse was trading in my jeans for baggy jailhouse trousers. Don't get me started on the shoes. They looked like the kind an old farmer would wear.

The walls were dull white brick, the gates and doors thick tempered metal alloys. My screen-less window was barred by a thick mesh of steel. Just beyond that were thick grey concrete columns. All this was meant to keep me from breaking out into the yard, which was surrounded by not two, but three enclosures of thirty-foot-high chain-link fencing, with rolls of razor wire, mounted on top. And if that didn't stop me, then the guard with the AR-15 semiautomatic rifle definitely would.

There were a whole lot of other Natives inside the razor-tipped gates of Drum. I wasn't keen on befriending them. Most of them belonged to gangs—a ruthless, violence-loving bunch. I had spent some years of my life on the rez and therefore knew the violence some of these young men were prone to. What with so many of them stemming from a violent upbringing. In Drum, these aggressive men lived to prey on the new and the weak, closing in on them like a pack of hungry hyenas.

Right off the bat, I was designated a medium-class security threat because my crime was of a violent nature. Other inmates didn't bother me much and didn't step on my toes, and vice versa. Sex offenders and rats, on the other hand, had it bad. Either beat downs or stabbings were in store for those unlucky few. I made a few friends here and there, but I chose to mostly stick to myself. I was never big into gambling, drugs, smoking, or any of that stuff, so I didn't create any debts or problems with any other inmates. I just did my time. Also, I strictly steered clear of the inside politics. But it was still prison, so I had to always watch my back.

During my two-year stint, I lost count of the lock-downs due to stabbings, overdoses, beat downs, and other suspicious group activity. A few deaths occurred during my stay, causing the prison to go on lockdown for up to a month. Luckily for me, I had a small pink wash basin, vital when we were only allowed to shower every ten days during lockdowns. A wash bin meant a good old-fashioned bird bath hand washing. I couldn't have asked for it better in those shithole circumstances.

Then one day, along came a nice, quiet fella. He had nowhere to sit for lunch, so my buddy and I invited him to take the extra seat at our table. His name was Willy. He hailed from Maskwacîs in central Alberta. He was a lifer. In prison, you don't ask what a man is in for. So I never asked, and he never told. The year sailed on. Willy and I became good friends. He had the look of a pow-wow singer, with a rounded face and long black flowing hair. His ponytail was always kept neatly tucked under his black Nike cap most of the time. His thick wireframe glasses gave him the look of a sophisticated man, and he was, to a point. He was very street-smart. Growing up on the rough and shattered streets of a gang-swarmed reserve town, you had to be. Willy and I became friends, at first, through our taste in music: heavy metal. I was, and always have been, big into the brash sounds of electric guitars and fast-paced drumming.

At Drum, most of the music that floated around was gangster Rap. I hated gangster Rap. So naturally, Willy and I traded and sold each other CDs, compact discs being the only form of music to acquire inside prison. I found myself constantly in his cell, listening to music, talking about life, and playing one another on his PlayStation. No, not PS5. The original PlayStation was the only gaming system allowed (along with N64). Drumheller Penitentiary was like going into the past, with no new-age internet-capable items available to us.

In due course, my new best friend and I got to talking about our personal lives, and he told me about his life on "the outs." He talked about how his father was killed, not even a year before he himself was incarcerated. His father, who had been an old-school metalhead and a Satanist, was stabbed to death at a rockers bar in the big city. During that conversation, I told Willy what I had done that got me locked up and how I could have been another statistic of a stabbing had it not been for my mixed martial arts training.

By that point in time, I figured we were close enough buddies, so I dared inquire about him. He looked at me solemnly and studied me for a brief moment. Then he said, "Second-degree murder, bro. I was drinking for about a week with some cousins and friends. Nothing but hard alcohol. So anyways, a cousin of mine had gifted me this knife earlier that night. A knife which my dad had originally gifted to him. It was totally a satanic knife, with a demon head nestled into the base of the handle, and some ancient runes and designs etched into the grip. I was thankful, but then ...." He rolled his eyes and punched his bed. "Then the fucker goes and says something about my younger half-sister. He said how he wouldn't mind going into her room that night to say hello while we were all passed out ...." Willy's expression changed.

"You okay, bro? You don't have to carry on," I said.

He threw me the "it's okay" gesture, puckered his lips, and carried on after a long weary exhale. "And then, I just don't know what happened to me. It's like everything went black. I remember getting super mad, and that was it. When I came to, I was staring into the dead face of my cousin, lying on the floor in a mess of his own gore. I guess I slit his throat. Blood was everywhere. Coming out of his neck, everywhere. Everybody ran from the house, except for my little brother. He dragged me out of the house, and we both took off in his car." Willy turned away.

I had to say something. All that I was able to muster up was, "Deep, bro. Deep."

Although this kind of story would no doubt make ordinary people walk out and not ever talk to that person again. I didn't. I wasn't about to judge this guy. Mistakes were made. Alcohol will do that.

So, we carried on with our friendship. I told him I'd lived near Maskwacîs as a kid. I was familiar with the area. My father was married up there in the town of Wetaskiwin. I told Willy that I stayed on the Louis Bull reserve and went to a public school out in the middle of the countryside, just west of there. He asked me what school, and I told him. He turned to face me with wide eyes and mouth agape.

"What's up?" I asked.

"That's where it is!" he said excitedly.

"Where what is?"

"The knife!"

"The knife?" I echoed, raising my eyebrow.

He told me that the school I went to as a kid was where he had buried the knife he killed his cousin with. The demon knife. He knew it would be vital evidence in his murder trial, so he and his brother floored it a half-hour, or so, west to bury it among the hills. Since the knife was once his late father's, he wanted to keep it as a memento, so he buried it in a spot where he would never forget, in the thick hedgerows of a countryside school yard. He kept the exact whereabouts from his brother, knowing the police would eventually demand the information. He then drew me a map of the precise location and told me if something ever happened to him, that I would dig it up and deliver it to his younger brother. I promised him, hoping I would never actually have to unearth the murder weapon.

Another year of friendship passed. We grew to be like brothers, Willy and me. He was a lifer, so he still had another ten years or so until his parole eligibility dates. Parole would be in the air if he was lucky.

I, on the other hand, was granted day parole two years after beginning my incarceration in Drumheller Penitentiary. I was transferred to a minimum-security institution to wait out my release date. And where was this place located? None other than on the sacred grounds of the Maskwacîs Cree Nation, Willy's hometown reserve. It was like a work camp. We had real bedrooms, cooked our own food, and weren't locked up all day. Best of all was that there were Elders there to help us on our healing journey. I loved the drastic change.

One day I was preparing my meal, and my housemate had the satellite TV tuned into the local 6 p.m. news program.

"Good evening," the reporter began. "We begin our broadcast with breaking news. Drumheller Institution is under lockdown after a man was stabbed in his cell. Authorities will keep the prison under full lockdown until they conclude their investigation. The name of the victim has been released: twenty-three-year-old William J. Knife was found alone in his cell with multiple stab wounds to his chest and abdomen. He is currently in critical condition at Drumheller General Hospital. He is not expected to survive ...."

My peripheral vision dimmed. I nearly fainted. I had just kicked it with him two weeks prior. I had said I would write to him within the month. My heart ached.

A MONTH OR SO PASSED, and I was finally out. Mia picked me up in my blue Audi. She looked more beautiful than ever, leaning on that hood. Screaming, she sprinted over to me and thrust her whole body on me. I held her firmly while she wrapped her legs around my torso and squeezed. She clasped onto my face and smothered me in kisses. She smelt of cinnamon and vanilla. I was in heaven.

"I've missed you so-o-o much, baby," she breathed into my ear.

"Mmm, I've missed you more," I replied.

"I love you so much."

Mia had never said she loved me before. I had fallen in love with her long ago. I was just afraid to ever say anything, so I waited for the right time to say it—if there ever would be a right time. Like at that very moment. "I love you, Mia. More than anything in the world," I said.

She stared into my eyes. "Hmmm, I dunno about that," she said and smiled widely.

"Wait, what?"

"Come on, let's go." She dismounted from our embrace and gripped me tightly by the hand. I followed her unquestioningly. She stopped just before she got to the car and whirled around. "You wanna drive?"

I thought for a moment. It had been about two years, and I knew I was probably rusty as hell. "No, babe. You drive," I said. "And what's this 'I don't know about that' talk?" She continued to grin slyly without saying anything, ducking swiftly inside the car through the driver's door.

I strolled around to the passenger side, lost in thought.

Once inside the car, Mia turned to me, and her smile grew. "So ... do you wanna meet your son?" Her eyes gestured at the backseat.

I whipped my head around to meet the beautiful gaze of our baby boy. My own flesh and blood. He had my face and his mother's nose. But best of all, he had her eyes. His own caramel irises sparkled vividly in the window-tinted sunlight. A stream of emotions flooded through me. I was truly at a loss for words.

"His name is Adrian. I named him after your late grandmother. He's just over a year old."

Right then and there, I knew what she meant by her sly comment. I had the best surprise any man can ever ask for: a beautiful, healthy baby boy.

I saw Mia once during a private visit early in my incarceration. After that, I told her it was too hard seeing her leave, so I wanted to wait until my parole to see her in person again. We kept in close contact through the phone and old-school love letters. Mia told me that my brother, sister, mother, and stepfather all reluctantly agreed to keep her pregnancy secret from me. In the wake of baby Adrian's birth, they all pitched in and helped Mia take care of him. My family wanted to give me the surprise of a lifetime. Literally. They all knew how much I loved Mia and even figured that I would love the surprise. My family knew me all too well.

MIA AND I HIT THE ROAD following our few moments of our new family's embrace. I wanted to be clear of the CSC grounds as soon as possible and never have to look back. Ever. We were minutes into our road trip heading south, and that was when I remembered the promise I had made.

"Babe, turn here. I need to make a stop. It's not too far out of the way." I pointed to a paved service road just off the reserve grounds. I knew exactly where it led to. I knew the area well, even though it had been several years since I'd been in the vicinity.

About half an hour later, we arrived at the elementary school. The main building rested just off the main highway, separated by a deep ditch, and surrounded by an array of tall hedgerows and aspen trees. It was July and, thankfully, void of any bustling student activity. I showed Mia where to park and scrambled out of the vehicle.

I leaned in the open door, eyed my sleeping son in the backseat and smiled, then turned to face my girlfriend. "I'll be right back, okay, babe?" Mia nodded slowly, looking a little confused.

The spot where Willy told me he had buried the knife was easy to find. It was just on the other side of a chest-high, chain-link fence, beneath a canopy of dense trees and shrubs. Way too close to the playground, I thought. I was astounded that it hadn't been unearthed by a curious student already. I dug wildly at the soil with my bare hands, probably looking like a rabid dog.

After a few minutes of wild excavating, my fingertips brushed the edges of something. I dug deeper and extracted a dirt-caked wad of cloth. I opened the cloth and uncovered a thick, rusty incense tin bound tightly with deteriorating duct tape. I was just about to begin peeling off the tape, when I heard the blast of a siren, the kind police cruisers emit when the cops want to grab your attention.

I put the tin back in the hole and dashed for the car.

"How are we today, sir?" asked an older sheriff, a little on the chunky side. I could feel him staring at me through his mirrored sunglasses.

"Not too bad, Sheriff. Yourself?" I asked.

"School's closed. Can I ask why you're parked here?"

I had to think fast. A little white lie was the answer.

"Well, actually, sir, my son goes to this school. And he just won't stop bugging me about a toy he lost here, so here I am in the middle of nowhere looking for the damn thing."

"Your son, huh? Well, here's the thing. According to your plates, you're not from around here."

Damn. I was busted red handed.

Another white lie. "Yes sir, that's correct. But for the time being, he stays with my mother and father just over in Louis Bull." I figured some real truth might lighten the mood, so I said: "I've actually just been released on parole. Like, today. From the minimum-security place just on the reserve."

The sheriff removed his sunglasses and stared at me boldly. "Is that right? Might you have a piece of valid identification?" His eyes were bloodshot. I handed him my only piece of identification: my Corrections Service Canada identification card.

"Okay, this should only take a moment," he said, sucking in his paunch and squeezing back behind the steering wheel of his cruiser. He picked up his radio handset and began speaking. I couldn't hear what he was saying.

A few minutes passed. The sheriff finally clambered back out of his vehicle and approached me. "Okay, my good sir, you're clear to go. But I advise you to be very careful. There was a"—he hesitated—"car accident just up the hill. Pretty grim. Be very cautious. Finish your search and be on your way." With that said, the sheriff nodded at me, wedged back behind the wheel of his car, and peeled out of the narrow, freeway-bordered parking lot.

I stood and waited until the sheriff was well enough away before scurrying back to my little excavation, but not before Mia gave me a hurry-the-hell-up honk of the car's horn. I could hear Adrian crying and yelling from the car like kids do when they're hot and hungry. I returned to the metal tin and carefully began removing the duct tape, which peeled off in decayed strips. For some reason, my hands were shaking. Finally, after about five minutes of impatient tinkering, I opened the box and peered inside.

The knife blade gleamed like a piece of raw, untouched gold. Not a single spot of damage or rust was visible. It was just as Willy had described it. The blade was meant to be pointed downwards, with the head of an uncanny, hellish creature resting at the top of the handle, its deformed head adorned with a crown of bulging horns. Beady eyes popped out of the menacing head like blood red jewels, its mouth fully agape with four sets of razor-tipped fangs. The handle was covered with engravings of some ancient-looking runes. The blade looked more like a spear tip than a dagger.

I shuddered just looking at the dreadful thing, but a promise was a promise.

I returned to the car with the tin in hand. Mia watched as I slid into the passenger seat. "Okay, what the heck was that all about, bud, and where the hell did you go?" she demanded.

"Just promised an old friend I'd deliver this to his kid brother," I answered, letting my breath catch up with me.

"What is it?"

I showed her quickly. Just a glimpse. Then I snapped the case tightly shut and tossed it into the glove box.

"Whoa—wait, wait. Can I have another look at that thing?" she said.

I fished out the covered knife and showed her again.

"Oh, my—no way. It can't be."

"What is it?" I asked.

"I swear to the life of me, my cousin showed me a knife exactly like that when I was a kid. She was all into this Satan worshipping and occult black magic stuff."

"Which cousin was this?"

"Tirana. But you wouldn't have known about her. She died when I was eight."

"Can I ask how?" I had a sinking feeling in my gut at that point.

"Some crazy asshole stabbed her to death. It was—"

It was like a black cloud obliterating the sun. "Sorry to cut you off, babe," I said, scrambling out of the vehicle. I stopped, half out the open door. "Do we still have that army trench tool in the trunk?"

"Oh ..." Mia thought for a moment. "You mean that

mini shovel thingy?"

"Yeah."

"Yes, it should still be back there. I've never touched it."

I finished heaving myself out of the car and bolted to the trunk.

Yes.

The "mini shovel thingy" was still there. I snatched it and went around to the open passenger door. I looked in at Mia. She was feeding Adrian cheerios one at a time. "I'll be just another five minutes. Again. Sorry, but believe me, it's for the best. I'll explain when I get back."

I returned to the spot where I had just excavated and scooped out the dirt, burrowing down a few feet more until sweat dripped from my forehead, stinging my eyes and splashing in the dirt. I didn't bother blanketing the knife this time, as Willy had done. I figured some damaging rust would be good for the knife.

Good for the world.

I tossed the vile thing in the hole and buried it once again, this time taking a few extra minutes to compact the dirt.

Illustration: Patricia Soop

EIGHT

THE LAST HOUSE

THE LONE HOUSE atop the wooded hill had been abandoned for years, but on this cloud-free evening, a candle burned in the window. Scanning through my field glasses, I knew there were people up there. I had once known this place very well. It used to be a safe haven well enough away from the rest of the "bad doings" of what was left of society.

Seated astride my saddled steed I let loose a heavy sigh and eyed my brother sideways. Maybe he couldn't yet see it. Couldn't tell. Couldn't feel. But I had noticed it long before the real effects started to take place, winding through his body and, most of all, his bones. And, sooner rather than later, his mind.

It was that last act—his own stupidity—that proved that the Indigenous Peoples of North America weren't exactly immune from the disease like they said. At best, we were resistant to the airborne strain. But direct contact with it that was a different story.

Bradley leaned over enough that it looked like he was ready to fall off his horse and call it quits, a sickly spew of black liquid discharging from his mouth. I dismounted and went to check on him.

"You okay up there?" I asked, making sure to approach from the opposite side of his horse, Cub, to avoid the puddle of black tar.

"Yeah, I'm good," he said, suppressing a wretched cough. He wiped his crusty mouth with the back of his dirty winter mitt. "Just need me a little breather is all. A couple hours at the most." He glanced at me, the sockets of his eyes deep and dark, and his sclera now exiled of all the healthy whiteness. What stared back at me was almost no longer my brother, but just another victim of the disease.

You can't bullshit a bullshitter ... we know there's gonna be nothing in there but old shit and unused everything, from dead bodies to rotting food to endless swarms of dust bunnies.

I winced, trying my best not to look like I was ready to puke up my own mess of that day's measly rations. "Yeah," I said half-heartedly, "let's find a place for the night. Looks like the evening is catching up to us anyway."

No one wants to be caught out in the middle of the wide-open prairies in the dark, especially on a new moon night. No one.

I peeked over my shoulder. The sun's rays were just sinking below the western skyline, the rolling hills about to steal back the day with it.

"Just up the hill, over there," I said, pointing up at balsam poplars with my good hand. I glanced at my opposite hand; I was terrified to even know what kind of infection was brewing beneath the three-day-old bandage. "Looks like we're going for that old ranch I told you about."

The lonely house could have been a mirage, and we, the lost and thirsty stragglers roaming the desert. A gravel path twisted its way up the hill, slithering through clusters of brown ad green foliage like a river through the jungle. I turned to see that my only companion— my only living family—was now on the outer reaches of death. His sunken cheeks and badly deteriorating skin said it all. It had been less than a full day after direct contact with the infected.

"Maybe they have water. Prolly a well somewhere in their big-ass backyard," I said, more to lift my own spirits.

"Don't kid yourself, guy. You can't bullshit a bullshitter," Bradley replied. He laughed softly, which seemed to pain him. "We know there's gonna be nothing in there but old shit and unused everything. Abandonment. From dead bodies to rotting food to endless swarms of dust bunnies. But, hey, it's a place to stay. A roof over our heads." He threw me the least reassuring thumbs up gesture.

I shrugged and furrowed my lips, choosing not to mention having seen candlelight in the house's picture window. "Screw it. Let's just get up there and have ourselves a look before it gets too dark out."

My brother faked another smile, bowed slightly, and gestured for me to take point.

From the lower, prairie expanse, the house seemed like a small farmstead. Now up-close-and-personal, we could see that it was grander—I had only ever ridden by it from a distance in the past, not wanting to disturb the tenants. Though partially crumbling in some of the painted areas, the once-upon-a-time lavishness was still evident. A wrap-around porch encircled the front half of the Cape Cod-style house. It was a full two stories, with an array of curtained windows, an attic or smaller third story with one single, cloudy and weathered gabled window staring unnervingly down at us.

"Nice frickin' house," said Bradley. His voice sounded strong again, which reassured me a little. But it wouldn't last. It never did when it came to the infected.

"Too nice," I added, staring into the house. "Here, bro." From the ground, I handed him our only worthwhile weapon: an old-fashioned six-shooter with two rounds left in the cylinder. If things got too bad, that was one for him and one for me. Using it on another human being was never really an option.

I untied my personal favourite, a rusty katana. "I'm going to go see if it's safe."

Bradley nodded, checked the firearm with shaking hands, and then nodded again. "Guess I'll just wait here," he added.

I imagined a visitor's lodge already set up for us newcomers. A welcome mat, the hearty scent of country chicken roasting over a firepit. The ripe air of pine cleaners staining the hardwood floors.

But no. Of course not.

What welcomed me was stale air and fungus, with a side note of fire-charred wood. Damaged furniture, strewn with even worse-looking blankets, lay scattered about the rotting wood flooring. People. Definitely people. I jabbed the creaky door all the way aside with the katana's blade and stepped across the threshold.

"Hello," I called out softly, my sword grasped tightly in both hands. "I'm just looking for a place to sleep, for me and my—my—my brother." I almost said "sick brother," but I caught myself in time. The word, sick would get you killed.

No reply came.

I let down my sword, my tense shoulders growing heavy. I raked my head around in search of the candle. Nothing of the sort caught my eye. I whispered out: "Well, I guess it's safe to camp for the ni—"

"Hi," said what sounded like a teenager.

I snapped my head around so hard it made my neck bones crackle. There was the candle I had been looking for: down the blackened hall was the face of a young teen, her blonde hair illuminated in the candlelight like an ocean of prairie grass in the summer sun.

"Hi," I said, dropping my attack stance.

"There's a man outside with a gun. Please don't hurt us," she said so softly that I had to resist the urge to ask her to speak up.

"No, no, no," I said, sliding my trustworthy katana into the sheath. I raised my hands, palms out in a gesture of gentle approach, and stepped into the shade of the hallway. "We would never do that. We're just looking for a place to stay for the night—you know, to be out of the open—and then we'll be on our way first thing in the morning."

She leaned sideways so her face was out of the candle's direct light, her head tipping back as though she was trying to peek over the living room's far-off windowsill. "Are those horses? I haven't seen a horse in a really long time."

"Would you like to meet them?" I asked politely.

Her face lit up as she hurriedly placed the candle

on the nearest table and darted to the open doorway. She stopped just short of the threshold, turning to stare at me. "I'm not allowed to go outside when Mama and Papa are away. You know, because of the bad people who are always out there."

I was more than aware of the bad people.

I cautiously walked up to her side. A cool wind had picked up and sliced through the trees, making the twists of branches look like an army of distorted beings thrashing in unfiltered shadows.

Theresa's eyes snapped all the way open. Her mouth dropped wide before she even spoke, her gaze flickering to me, and then to my brother.

A shiver ran up my spine, and I felt we were being watched.

"Come on," I said, urging the girl to step back inside the house. "I'll be right back. I'm just going to go and check on my brother and the horses."

THE GIRL, watched from the dirty picture window as I helped Bradley dismount then hitched the horses to the solid railing. I propped Bradley up against a tree and I had to keep gazing over my shoulder to make sure no one was about to lunge at us. I securing the horses and caressed their smooth noses. I hated having to leave them out in the darkness, but I felt at least a little safer knowing we were no longer in the lower grasslands. And besides, the horses would alert us to incoming intruders.

"Goodnight, you guys," I whispered as I took one last look at the horses in the dim rays of dusk. I threw Bradley's arm around my shoulders and we headed inside.

"Who are you?" asked Bradley, his face twisting in pain as he limped to the dust-covered sofa and plopped himself down.

"We're Deacon and Bradley," I informed her. The girl introduced herself as Theresa, her glance switching back and forth from us to the horses.

"Are they okay?" she asked.

"They'll be fine. They're all watered up and cozy. Just like us," I joked.

I was ready to join my brother on the couch when the lone candle flickered violently as though someone had just tried to blow it out.

Theresa's eyes snapped all the way open. Her mouth dropped wide before she even spoke, her gaze flickering to me, and then to my brother. "Ma, Pa. They're back," she whispered excitedly. She rocketed out of her chair and bolted down the unlit hall. I hadn't heard a door open or shut. A nervous rush of needles carved through me, I looked at my rusty katana resting on the table and thought of the worst. Dare I pick it up and ready myself for an armed confrontation?

I remained quiet as my body froze up, my eyes landing on my brother, sleeping contentedly. He was my older brother, and I'd always gone to him for advice.

"Deacon!" Theresa's voice snapped me to my senses. "Are you coming?" Theresa hollered. It sounded like she was in the basement.

"Bro," I said, even though I knew Brad wouldn't hear me. He was out cold and would be until morning. "Brad, I'll be right back." I walked towards the black hall and stopped, my vision once more drawn to the old katana. Something inside me screamed at me to pick it up—as it always did when my neck hairs stood on end— but I fought against it, knowing the blade would only bring animosity to whoever was down there.

"Yeah," I called out. "I'll be right there. Just tucking in my brother." I composed myself and crept down the dark corridor as silently as possible. My racing heart slowed a touch as I rounded a corner into flickering light from down in the basement. I breathed a sigh of relief and headed down the stairs.

With wide eyes pinned to the growing flickers of light, I didn't see the rotten step. My foot smashed through the ruined tread, and I would have toppled face first had I not grabbed a hold of the rails.

I heard a loud gasp "Oh my God, are you okay?"

I jerked my head up to see Theresa standing at the bottom of the staircase, lit by the glow of candles.

I giggled, half out of nervousness and half out of relief at having caught myself before I tumbled. I tried to look past her and see what it was that I was stumbling unknowingly into. "Yeah, Theresa, I'll be okay. Just these old stairs almost killing me."

"Yes, sir," said another voice. A stout male voice. "Things around here have been falling apart for some time now. I hope you're okay." The man stepped out from the shadows and stopped behind Theresa, placing a fatherly hand on her slender shoulders. "Come on, Bradley."

Theresa turned abruptly; the candle cupped in her hand nearly snuffing itself with the sudden movement. "No, Dad," she giggled, "Bradley is the brother asleep upstairs. This one is Deacon."

The man snickered. "Oh, okay. Deacon, then." He

walked around his daughter and stuck out a welcoming hand. "My name is Albert. Of course, you've already met Theresa. Come, let me give you a hand." With that said, he stepped up a few of the stairs and waited as I grabbed hold of his wrist and used him as leverage to free my foot.

Rubbing my throbbing shin, I straightened up and took in my surroundings. Plain and simple, it was a home, not a shanty, broken-down palace that the main floor otherwise implied. An aged stove with a small flame sat in the centre of the living space. Beautifully kept furniture lined the floors. Oh, and the floors, how magnificently clean they were. I hadn't seen floors that clean for years upon filthy years. The reflection of the small flame inside the stove danced across the hardwood like a midnight moon on the open ocean. I scanned the upper walls, where the windows were well covered with layers of old towels and sturdy wood framing—good to keep in the light. Well done. The paint was faded and chipped, but where was there in this broken world to purchase new paint supplies?

"Wow. Very nice," I said. "Homey."

"Thank you," replied Albert. "Please, make yourself at home," he said, pulling out a chair from under a table and gesturing for me to sit.

"Sure," I said. As I sat, I could feel another pair of eyes scrutinizing me. "Is there—"

"Hello there," said a female voice. A woman stepped from the shadows of the unlit basement and greeted me graciously, a large plate in her hand. "You must be hungry," she said.

I eyed the plate in the woman's hands, my stomach immediately throwing itself into a fit of hungry growls. "I could eat," I said.

The woman seemed to float toward me, her feet making no sound and her legs barely seeming to move under her dress. "Here you go, darling," she said, placing the plate onto the table to my right. "My name is Carlina," she said. "Now, please. Eat."

I couldn't have cared less what kind of meat it was. Meat was meat. The body needs protein to survive. But then my brother came to mind. "Wait," I blurted out. "My brother. I'm pretty sure he'd like something to eat too."

Theresa spoke up. "Yes. Bradley. The one sleeping upstairs." She glanced at her mother sharply, her eyes darting to her father as he had his back to us, attend-

---

"This place. This place is like nothing else in this world. This place is ... magical.

What I am about to tell you is—"

A scream pierced the night.

---

ing to the fire. "Dad?" she asked in a low tone. "Can his brother come down too?"

Albert swung around. His eyes stayed put on mine. "How sick is he?"

"I don't know, Papa. He—"

"Very sick," I interjected. My heart sunk as I realized the truth. "I don't think he has even a few days left—if he's even lucky enough to survive the night." My head dropped.

"Theresa," said Albert. "Go check on this boy. If he's well enough to walk down here, bring him."

Without question Theresa bolted up the stairs, her naked feet slapping on the bare wood. For an odd reason, I was disturbed by her light footfalls across the floor above my head.

I realized this man was willing to help, with whatever kind of help was permitted to my ailing, half-dead brother. "Thank you," I said.

Carlina glided across the glazed floor and took a seat beside the fire, the sofa making a light crunching sound as she made herself comfortable. She then stared at me head-on, another smile forming across her lips. As warm as she seemed to be, I still felt there was more than meets the eye.

"So," I said, doing my best to ease my own mind. "This place is nice. How is it that you're able to keep up such a comfortable home?"

Smile not letting up, Carlina eyed her husband. I glanced at Albert. He took the limelight, dramatically stoking the fire once more before turning to face me. He had the air of a grand sorcerer about to recite the final words to a great spell. The fire roared to life as he bent his head back and stared at the ceiling. He cleared his throat. "This place. This place is like nothing else in this world. This place is ... magical. What I am about to tell you is—"

A scream pierced the night.

"What the hell was that!?" I leapt to my feet. It hadn't sounded like a human's scream.

Theresa hightailed up the stairs like a spooked animal.

"Papa, Mama," she wailed, "I think he's dead."

Albert bolted up the stairs two at a time. I was right on his heels.

"He's not dead, but he's damn close to it," said

Albert, his words coming to me like he was speaking underwater.

All I could do was stare in disbelief.

"He's gonna be alright," said Theresa, her hands tugged at my dirty sleeves.

I snapped my attention to her. "How the hell is he going to be alright?"

"No," interrupted Albert, getting off his knees. "There is a way."

I gaped at him. Were they all mad? Couldn't they see?

"Remember what I was saying about this place?" Albert said. "Go down and wait."

As I positioned my foot on the top stair, I looked again at my brother. He looked about a hundred years old. His lips were twisted into a hideous grin.

"Do what you can," is what I said.

TIME CREPT TO A SNAIL'S PACE. I wasn't sure what was going on upstairs, but I hoped my brother would be alive and well in the morning.

As if she read my thoughts, Carlina gently said, "Your brother will be just fine."

I couldn't take it anymore. I rose from my chair and began pacing. Minutes passed, I don't know how many, before I heard the footfalls of people coming down into the basement. Theresa was first, then Albert, followed by no one. My heart stopped.

"He's dead, isn't he?" I whimpered.

"No," answered Albert, glancing back at the stairs. "He's not."

A tall, sturdy man I knew as my brother came to the top of the stairs. It was as though ten years had been knocked off his age. His skin was flawless. Not a single indication of the disease.

"Bradley, is that you?" I whispered. "Is that really you?"

"It is," said Bradley. He sounded strange. The voice was his, but also not his, almost feral.

I swung around and faced Albert. "But how?"

"Like this," Bradley said.

I turned again to find my brother standing right in front of me, insatiable hunger burning in his eyes. He took one step back and opened his mouth; two razor-sharp fangs emerged where his canine teeth should have been.

He said, "Will you join us?"

186

NINE

THE EDGE
OF DARKNESS

H E SAT PATIENTLY at the steel interview table, drumming his fingers on its cold surface. His eyes darted around the room while he tried to find any sort of comfort in the fluorescent-lit, windowless room.

"Are we gonna be in this room very long?" he asked with bitter patience.

"Umm, let me just ... there we are. Now we're ready to get going," said the doctor. She wore a white lab coat with a bright red satin shirt beneath. She hit a button on a small handheld recorder, placed it standing upright on the table like a domino and readied her pen with a click. She smiled and nodded at the young man sitting before her, revealing her absolute readiness.

"You didn't answer my question," he said. He was young, still in the prime of his adolescence.

The doctor looked up at him from the upper rims of her thick-framed glasses. "Not long." She returned to her writing pad.

"Okay, good, 'cause this room is making me feel way too uncomfortable."

The doctor began speaking into the handheld recorder, "This is Dr. Emilia Santos with the Saley Regional Psychiatric Hospital. I am ready to begin session one with my patient, Mr. Lucas Matthew Willows. The time is," she glanced at her watch, "just past 1400 hours on November 15, 2022."

Lucas grinned. He relished the idea of having "mister" inserted before his name. It gave him a satisfied feeling, like a small warmth of fire brewing inside his cold, deep ocean of a heart. Usually, he had only ever been referred to as "mister" when a scolding was headed his way.

"Are you ready to start, Lucas?" asked Dr. Santos.

Lucas nodded, his eyes still darting around the padded room, its paint scheme a pale whiteness. He focused on an object in the top corner of the small cube of a room. A small, closed-circuit camera branched out from the wall and was aimed directly at the table at which he and Dr. Santos sat. His wandering gaze landed on the shadow of the recording device propped between them, and then his own shadow, cast diagonally across the metallic table.

Shadows.

He hated shadows.

"Let's begin by asking you, and please, answer to the best of your knowledge. What happened that night of the party? What led to you committing the acts which resulted in you ending up here?"

"Do you have anything to drink?" asked Lucas, his eyes once more affixed to the small camera with a blinking red light situated below the lens.

"Can you please make eye contact with me when we speak?" the young doctor asked.

Lucas's eyes settled coldly on Dr. Santos'

cinnamon-coloured irises. "A drink."

"Yes. Here, I've got some bottled water." She placed her pen down and reached into one of the pockets of her baggy lab coat, pulling out a plastic bottle.

"No, no, no." He smacked the table with an open hand in rhythm with his words. "That's not what I meant when I said 'drink,'" he said, a hint of something dark in his voice.

"Mr. Willows. That kind of beverage is strictly forbidden. Especially in your case, and above all in this place."

Lucas felt a speck of rage start to rise. The way the doctor had said "mister" had felt devious and made him think about the Cunninghams and the Grims. He focused and coerced his brain to calm the looming rage that had landed him here in the first place. "Should I start from where it all began?"

"Yes, Mr. Will—"

"Please, for our own sake. Just call me Lucas from here on out," he said sharply, trying his best to keep the brewing fire of hate under wraps.

"Okay then, Lucas. Now, let's have you start from the very beginning. That way we can start to understand your condition and therefore begin to help you."

Lucas had seen enough movies starring the crazy person as the lead character to know that they couldn't really help him. But he felt as though he had a lot of pressure on his conscience, and therefore, revealing the truth might help.

Dr. Santos tapped her pen lightly on the steel table. "Are we ready to start?" she asked.

"Okay," he exhaled, "Here's where it all began—"

* * *

I WAS BORN INTO ALCOHOLISM. I know it sounds cliché, but in my case, it wasn't. My birth mother never told me this, but I had a twin. They said that the other, my brother, died in the womb due to complications resulting from my mother's constant drinking in the first few months of her pregnancy with me ... and him. Father beat her every time he saw her put a bottle to her lips, which didn't help the pregnancy either. And to make matters worse, Dad was a raging alcoholic himself, picked up from years and years of abuse from both of his own parents and the residential school staff.

*I was removed from my party-loving parents'
home and placed in the foster care system
under the supervision of a white family.*

Mother was very pretty, from what I can remember. She had long black hair that glimmered in the lowest of lighting. And high cheekbones, just like pretty Indian women in the movies. She was tall, a trait that ran in our side of the family, especially in the women.

Dad was once a handsome man. Years of over-drinking eventually did a number on his chiselled good looks. After he was kicked out of the army and rejected by the RCMP, he became a passionate drinker, much more so than in his early teenage years. Bouts of rage were the results of Dad's "blackouts." I was often forced to flee and hide for hours on end out of fear for my life.

Not long after my seventh birthday, I was taken. A concerned parent of one of my schoolmates thought she recognized my parents out in public, wasted out of their heads of course. Said concerned parent glimpsed me while I waited patiently out in the parking lot in a hot car. Shortly after her disturbed phone call to the authorities, I was removed from my party-loving parents' home and placed in the foster care system. Then I was under the supervision of some white family named Cunningham.

Cunningham. A name that will forever be a thing of hatred in my heart and soul. I have no idea who the foster administration hires to do all the approving, but they sure do a bang-up rotten job picking the families that get to take care of us.

I was thrown into a large family of eight. I say thrown because that's what it literally felt like soon after the system took me in. No one in the foster system's administration sector really seemed to bat an eye at me; they just wanted me out of their hair as soon as possible.

The Cunningham family had two older kids of their own making. Jared was nine, and Janet was thirteen. The other three were foster children. I was the sixth addition. In no time at all, I found out that the father was a hard-drinking, cocaine-loving son-of-a-bitch prone to violent outbursts. The mother was nothing but a giant baby who cowered and obeyed the father's every sick demand. Instead of hearty meals, we got mostly food bank rejects and cheap microwave dinners. The rest of the government's handout money either went up the father's nose or seeped down his throat. And oh boy, did he ever love bringing the good old drunken backhand to his wife. She was so busy trying to win his love, she didn't care anything about the children—with the exception of her own offspring, of course.

The Cunningham's own two children, Jared and Janet, were real-life demons. Literally. They were the only two of us who were actually fed and clothed somewhat well. They also had their own bedrooms. I can't say that much for us foster kids—the government cash cows.

One summer day, I was confined out back in the Cunninghams' backyard, digging some trenches for my toy soldiers. Out of nowhere comes Jared with his overgrown size 8 shoes, all the while screaming in his croaky, big boy voice: "Bigfoot attacking!" He roared loudly as he stomped on my only toys, leaving them in a heap of green plastic shards. He laughed as he did it. The salt in the wound was him kicking dirt in my face and then punching me in the kidneys.

While I was hunched over trying to find my breath, Jared leaned in and whispered coldly: "Dontchu go squealing this to Ma or Pa. They wouldn't give two shits about a scrawny little Indian kid like you anyways."

And that's just one instance of far too much suffering under Jared to count. Yet it's not even the worst.

Then there was Janet. Oh, Janet. Let's just say she was some kind of an adolescent succubus, far from the angel Mrs. Cunningham made her out to be. On more than a few occasions, I was sexually violated by this "angel" named Janet. I was made to do sick and unspeakable things that involved her crotch and other body parts. Every few nights, she would come into our bedroom while the rest of the house was sound asleep and begin her sexual perversions by kidnapping one of us away from our sleep and slipping us into her own bed. My foster brother Brett and I were chosen more frequently than Thomas because we were both Indigenous. Janet held a deep fondness for our naturally tanned skin.

My corrupted soul dwelled in that true-life hellhole for over two years until, one day, I decided I'd had enough. I ran away and never looked back. At nine years old, kids don't know how to survive on the streets, but I did. Two years of fending off two demonic "siblings" had taught me how to cope well in the unforgiving streets of the inner city.

Before long, I was taken in by a homeless couple by the names of Peter and Anika, a down-and-out immigrant couple. They had come across me wandering the streets in a state of utter hopelessness, my tired eyes and frail body in need of nourishment. Though they had almost nothing, they treated me well compared to the Cunninghams. Anika, especially, made me her main priority when it came to the small scraps of food we managed to locate.

I can't really recall how long I stayed with Peter and Anika. Nobody had a watch or a working clock. We stayed in—to some degree—a relatively well-made house in a secret shanty town located in an old, immense, burnt-out metal manufacturing plant. Only the well-con-structed metal shell still stood undamaged after years of neglect, which was good enough protection from the winter elements. Amid an economic recession, the city didn't want to spend time and money to clean up the old building. With the economy's downfall at the time, no companies were in line to purchase the dilapidated structure and the massive plot of land it stood upon. For the second time in my young life, I was in the middle of a desperate domestic situation.

One night I decided to take a stroll. My curious, pre-teen self had never seen such a large building before. Not every section of the abandoned warehouse was inhabited; there were spots full of black mould and toxic industrial sludge. Lying smack in the middle of the build-ing was a mountain of trash, mostly burnt-out chunks of rubber and steel. With my nine-year-old curiosity getting the best of me, I thought I would try my hand at climbing it. Reaching the top, I came across a body, just lying there, a head of dishevelled grey peeking out from an old ratty sleeping bag. Thinking I had come across a corpse, I held my tongue and started scrambling back down the mound.

"Now, just you hold up there, young'un," said a raspy voice.

I stopped and whirled around. "Who are you?"

He rose to a wobbling seated position. "Hell, I'm one of you'se. Just having me a little drink is all," he said, brandishing a dark bottle. "Would you like some?"

"What is it?"

"Come now," he said, waving me over. "You like grape juice, dontcha?"

I was nine years old, so of course, I loved grape juice. "Yeah, I do." I rushed to his side, snatched the bottle with both hands and slugged back a gulp without hesitation. Straightaway the contents came coursing back up. After a bout of sickness, I scrambled back down the trash mound, my new friend, whose name I never acquired, laughing at me while he stayed put where I'd found him.

My head felt light. I was finally able to understand why my father loved the bottle so much. Feeling like I was somehow out of my own skin, but in a good way, I made my way around the rest of the massive steel building, curious as to who else lived there. I stumbled across the dirt and frost-caked ground, enjoying songs issued from the main encampment in the far corner and laughed at nothing in particular. The "town" we called it. For once in my life, I didn't feel lonesome. I felt great and was seeking out someone my own age to share the feeling with.

At last, I staggered to a dead end, where the uneven

wall merged with the uneven dirt. Shadowy figures crept all around me, but I wasn't afraid. My keen eyes caught sight of movement in what was probably once a guardhouse, a deserted guardhouse overtaken by gloom and ice.

"Hey," I yelled. "Any other kids in there?" I heard slight movement. I took a step inside the guardhouse through the small doorless frame. Pure darkness greeted me, my steamy breath vanishing into the icy black.

"Come in," said a voice from the dark. I couldn't tell if it was a woman, man, adult, or even a teenager. The voice was low-pitched and throaty, almost a growl, like someone who'd smoked three packs a day for the past twenty years. The guardian of this place, I assumed.

"But I can't see anything. I could poke my eyes out or worse."

"Then why not just reflect the light from the outside?" it replied. "Use the mirror right next to you."

I badly wanted a new friend. My eyes having somewhat attuned to the dimness, I spotted a mirror resting against the unhinged door. I stepped to it and grabbed hold, my small fingers losing grip in the cold. I stood there, and it fell to the frozen ground.

SMASH! The glass shards exploded everywhere in the dark room.

"Oh no, I'm so sorry!" I blurted out, terror bubbling up in my throat. "I didn't mean to break your mirror." I felt the cold eyes of the hidden guardian staring back at me from the dark. But he or she didn't scold me. "I'll go if you want me to. I'll understand."

Still no response from within. I took the silent treatment as my cue to go away.

Later that evening, following a few rounds of "grape juice" tasting and whiskey shooting among the adults, there was an exchange of blows between Peter and one of the vagrant men over who should get the first bite of a donated turkey. The vagrant lost the scuffle and ran to the police, and they showed up to disperse our gathering. They flattened our homes and trashed our only possessions. In fear of what would happen to me, I ran for dear life again.

I found an old tent and ducked inside. There was a raggedy old bed inside, and beside the bed was a large, spotless mirror. For a moment, I thought of using this one to replace the one I had broken in the guardhouse, but I hadn't seen my own reflection in weeks. So I stepped up to the mirror for a look. What I saw in the mirror wasn't my own reflection; I saw only shadows moving behind me. I spun around, but there was nothing else in there with me. Spurred on by terror, I bolted from the tent.

When the police found me trying to climb back up the mountain of rubber and steel, they took me in and pitched me back into the good old foster care system. I was once again thrown back to the dogs.

THE NEW HOME was a large house that sat perched overlooking the deep slicing bluffs of a river valley. The house was old. The roof was steep, sloped, and pointed like an old Victorian dwelling. The siding was decrepit old wood that was crumbling off in pieces, and the paint inside was bland.

It was at this new home where I met my new foster sister, Meredith. Meredith and I were made to sit and kneel every evening in front of a statue of an emaciated man hanging on a wooden cross. We had to speak words I didn't fully comprehend. I once asked my new foster mother, Mrs. Grim (I will call her Grim for I can't remember or even pronounce her real surname), "Who is that hungry-looking man nailed to the cross?" My answer was a clout across the lips and a scolding. "There will be no blasphemy in my house. Especially from a little sinner like you." For the third time in my young life, I was amidst a hopeless situation.

Mrs. Grim was a true Catholic crusader from Spain. She had spent a number of her young adult years as a missionary in the unforgiving jungles of South America, where she taught underprivileged Indigenous kids like me. I often wondered if that was where she devised her hatred for people like me. I was still only around ten or eleven years old.

For some unknown reason, Mrs. Grim's husband was rarely home.

Meredith and I were sent to bed every night at 8 p.m. on the dot. We were homeschooled daily in the run-down, spider-infested basement of Mrs. Grim's house. I wouldn't have even dared to call it schooling. Besides a little actual educational learning, all we really did for months on end was recite and memorize verses from the Bible. "The only book that matters in life," as Mrs. Grim put it. I vividly recall my birth mother telling me some very detailed accounts of her rigorous upbringing in the residential school system. Nuns and Catholic teachers from her stories resembled Mrs. Grim and her strict, fanatical ways. Mrs. Grim even wore a black veil like the nuns from my mother's stories.

If Meredith and I weren't being schooled on the bible then we were cleaning the house, from top to bottom, for hours on end. "Cleanliness is next to Godliness" was another thing Mrs. Grim liked to say to us as we scrubbed.

In the upper recesses of Mrs. Grim's house, there was a locked room that was strictly off limits. One early winter evening, the howling wind trying to break through the windows, I was upstairs, cleaning the spiral staircase. Mrs. Grim was up to something inside the off-limits room behind the dead-bolted door. I heard muffled voices emanating from inside the room; it sounded like she was conversing with someone—or something.

SMASH.

I had been so focused on trying to hear what Mrs. Grim or her conversation partner were saying behind that thick door that I flinched when I heard a deafening crash of plates breaking on the kitchen hardwood downstairs. In an instant, Mrs. Grim stormed out of the room to get downstairs and initiate a punishment to Meredith for breaking her cherished china.

I was on the top step scrubbing the bare hardwood as she rushed past me. I glanced up and down the hall and noticed she had forgotten to tightly close the door to the secret room. It slowly creaked open as I stared. It was my one and only opportunity. I went for it, without hesitation.

The room was dark and cold. It was the early onset of an icy winter, and the room felt as though every heating vent was closed. I tried the stiff light switch, but it didn't have any power. It was as if the room was meant to be isolated from any kind of energy influence from the rest of the house.

Perched in the central zone of the house was a huge crystal chandelier. It was like the sun in the inner circle, and the rest of the house was the solar system, which revolved around it. I remembered the guardhouse in the shantytown and how a mirror had reflected light into the dark space. So, I bolted into Meredith's and my room and grabbed the hand mirror off the dresser. I positioned it so that the vivid light from the chandelier down the hall reflected off the mirror, and shone illumination into the far room. Voila. Problem solved.

First things first, I crept and waited at the top of the central spiral stairs, listening to hear if Mrs. Grim was still scolding Meredith. She was. I could even hear the slapping of the long flat punishment stick against the bare skin of my thirteen-year-old foster sister. Meredith's light whimpering meant Mrs. Grim had only just begun; she usually didn't stop until we were yelping like terrified pups—pleading for her to stop. I had a few valuable minutes to spare.

I dashed back on tiptoe to the forbidden room. I stopped and lightly pushed the door open. It creaked like a small animal in pain. I hated that sound, not only because it gave me the creeps but because it could betray my taboo action. If discovered, I would be next under the stick and would be forced to spend a few nights alone in the cold, damp basement.

I stopped to have a listen before carrying on.

Mrs. Grim was speaking in her stern, brassy voice, which reverberated all the way up to the second-storey corridor. Chills ran up my spine. "God will not have Diablo's bride living under this roof. You will learn that, mija," she said with her firm accent.

While I stood in the doorway, waiting to hear if Mrs. Grim was still occupied with Meredith, my eyes slowly adjusted to the darkness of the barely lit bedroom. The room's layout was exactly like our own, except there was only one bed, instead of two, at the far end near a boarded-up window. The bed was dishevelled; its bedding wrinkled as though it had been recently slept in. A bulky wardrobe sat in the far corner looming by itself like an eternal shadow. I was reminded of the monsters I had only ever dreamt about. On the side of the room near the door was a wooden table with a lone wooden chair. I skulked to the concealed window to try to shed some more light into the room, but it was securely boarded up.

Unlike the small mirror Meredith and I shared, the secret bedroom had a full-sized vanity mirror hanging on the wardrobe door. Still on the tips of my toes, I stepped in between the mirror and the ray of chandelier light seeping into the room from down the hall. I could not for the life of me see my physical reflection.

Come here right now, boy," she screamed
as she raced across the floor toward me,
her long dressing gown making her
look like a floating, lurching nun.

I took another step forward for a closer examination of the blackened glass. I touched what should have been cold glass with the tips of my fingers. The glass was warm as if some heat source radiated behind it ... or inside it. Then as I strained my eyes to see better in the dark, something moved in the mirror. My heart started racing. But at least I knew I wasn't a vampire or dead as a ghost—as they say about not seeing your own mirror image.

Suddenly, Meredith squealed like a pig being chased by a hungry wolf. The sound of her agony shot a shiver tearing up my spine. I knew Mrs. Grim would be done and on her way back upstairs. I made sure I had not jiggled the wardrobe mirror out of place, and as quietly as possible, I crept back across the room and out into the hall, slowly pulling the door closed behind me and putting the hand mirror behind my back. The room was so cold that my breath puffs were visible in the light as I closed the door with a click.

"What are you doing, mijo?" snapped Mrs. Grim.

She was standing at the top of the landing, her cold eyes glued to me like I was about to be dead prey, hanging by her clenched fangs. I thank my lucky stars she did not notice the hand mirror I had sequestered behind my back.

"Just closing the door, señora. You accidentally left it open. I will get back to my duties now," I said as I backed away. I felt as though I had been trapped under icy water fighting for my breath.

"Snooping around in my off-limits room? Betraying my trust in a Christian house of the Lord, are we?" she barked in a malicious tone that seemed to claw its way out from the abyss of her deep, ominous innards.

"No, ma'am. I—I was just closing the door is all. I swear to G—" I stopped myself.

"Lies and blasphemy. And in my house? Oh, we will see about that, won't we? Come here right now, boy," she screamed as she raced across the floor toward me, her long dressing gown making her look like a floating, lurching nun. The hand mirror fell to the floor and smashed into shards as she grabbed me by the ears and dragged me down the stairs into the basement.

SHIVERING UNCONTROLLABLY, I tried to assure myself that everything was going to be okay. My ears throbbed, but that was the least of my problems in that basement. I was lucky to have found a tattered blanket under the stairs, but nonetheless, my body ached from the cold and damp. Huddled in a corner of the bare greyness, I hoped that what was left of my body warmth would stay with me through the night. It didn't.

For a woman with a lot of useless belongings and such a big house, Mrs. Grim sure kept the basement deserted and barren as an abandoned prison. I imagined Alcatraz and dungeons. There was absolutely nothing for me down there to even use as bedding. I felt like I had been thrown into solitary confinement. All I could do was curl myself up in a ball and tremble hopelessly in the corner of that dusty crypt.

To make matters worse, I was alone. Too alone. My hazy thoughts were the only thing keeping my mind off the blistering coldness biting at the skin of my exposed head and feet.

Cold, are we?

I heard the voice clearly; it bounced off the walls of my dungeon with a little echo. It was a full-bodied, robust voice, not anything like the little voice in your head is supposed to be. It was my own voice.

I wondered if I was starting to lose my mind from the constant shivering and feeling of bleakness.

Here, let me help you. I heard myself say. Not keen on succumbing to hypothermic madness, I squeezed my eyes closed tightly.

Help. No?

"How are you gonna help me?" I finally replied.

Like this.

I felt a blast of hot air burst across my back.

How's that?

I embraced the warming flare-up all over my body. Had I not been made to fear God so much, I would have sworn that He had performed one of his so-called miracles. In no time, I was fast asleep and dreaming that I was on a horse, a mighty, gleaming black steed. Its hooves were thick and feathery, and we shook the ground as we thundered across a wide meadow. I was perched comfortably on its broad saddled back feeling a warm summer breeze sweep across my face. Suddenly the steed stopped, and I went flying through the air, hitting a large tree trunk dead on. My face instantly felt numbing pain spread from ear to ear.

"Up with you, mijo. It is time to go and repent for your sins." I heard the raspy voice cut right through my dream before my eyelids snapped open just as she slapped me across the face again.

"Okay, okay, I'm up!" I screamed. My voice seemed to fill the entire basement.

Mrs. Grim gaped at me, eyes wide and full of absolute shock. I had never once raised my voice to her like that. She immediately stopped hitting me, spun around, and stormed across the empty floor and back up the stairs.

That's how it's done. I heard my own voice again, although I hadn't spoken. I pushed myself to my feet, dusted myself off, and went upstairs to face the day.

My outburst of defiance wasn't long-lived. I may have thought I had Mrs. Grim on the ropes. Was I ever wrong. I was relegated to the large backyard. I had been living at the Grim household for many months and not once had I been permitted to see the backyard—until then. It was like a jungle, an overgrown, out-of-control jungle. Weeds and vines grew right out of the concrete of a large terrace, looking like Mayan temple grounds. Unsightly weeds had overtaken any flower beds that may once have been cultivated. Massive trees stood row on row like giants standing tall—giants with hair badly in need of a trim.

Hidden in that jumble of trees was an army of wasps

that decided they would move in on Mrs. Grim's jungle. I was told to destroy their homes. The battle went immediately awry.

It's a good thing I wasn't allergic to wasps. Almost immediately, I was cut down by their deadly weapons. Too many stings to count. I dropped like a soldier in battle, taken out by machine gun fire. A machine gun barrage of deadly stingers.

I AWOKE IN THE HOSPITAL with almost no recollections of my defeat in battle. My face felt bloated, and it was. All in all, I had been stung a total of eighteen times in my face, neck, and chest. Luck was with me; I didn't die. Meredith had called 911, I would later learn.

"How are you doing, little brother?" asked Meredith, her piercing black eyes radiating sisterly fondness. She and I had been through a lot with Mrs. Grim in the past few months, and we found comfort in calling each other brother and sister. Her sweet face was the first for me to wake up to. The only one. It was just the two of us in that lonely hospital room.

Mrs. Grim was nowhere to be seen.

Meredith always reminded me of Wednesday Addams from The Addams Family TV show. She was very pale, half Asian and half white. Her jet-black hair was often plaited in two braids that dangled at the sides of her head and hung down past her slender shoulders. Mrs. Grim insisted that "Indian women" should wear braids to distinguish themselves from the rest of regular society—even though Meredith wasn't Indigenous. Her parents had passed away in a car crash when she was a toddler. Just like me, she had no other family, so she was thrown into the foster care system at the tender age of four.

"Where is—"

"She's not here," Meredith cut in. "She dropped me off a little while ago and told me to call her to pick us up once you're well enough to be discharged." She spoke briskly until she ran out of breath.

"How did I get here?" I asked.

"Oh God, Lucas," she expressed with both sadness and fear, "you should have seen her. After I heard your cries for help, I came running outside to see her already standing above you." She paused and waited for my reaction.

I nodded, urging her to go on.

Tears welled in her eyes. "She was smiling, Lucas. Oh God, how hideous that smile was."

My mind and soul felt like I'd been dealt another blow by a huge stinger. I slammed my head back onto my thin hospital pillow and stared up at the blank white ceiling. My head began to swim. Your foster mother would be happier to see you dead. She deserves to die, said the voice in my head. In no time, I dozed off from the mixture of numbing drugs and distressful news.

In the dead of the night, I awoke suddenly. Meredith was sleeping soundly in the padded armchair next to my bed. Moonlight far beyond the half-drawn window curtains slipped into darkness as a huge cloud drifted into its path. I froze up in fear at the sight of a large shadow standing directly behind her. My body seized up like a statue from a state of ice-cold fright and shock, unable to move a single muscle. I don't remember falling back asleep, but Meredith was gone the next time I opened my eyes.

The next day, the doctor decided I was well enough to return home. Home. If I could even call it that.

Meredith came back up to my room to inform me

that Mrs. Grim was outside waiting for us in her station wagon. I informed her that I'd be right down. First, I had to make a pit stop at the bathroom. The hospital bathroom was beyond creepy. It reeked of stale urine and disinfectant.

While I stood above the toilet draining my bladder, I deliberated over how many people—dead or alive—had sat on that exact same lump of porcelain.

The bare fluorescent light droned and flickered as though it was about to give out at any moment. Shuddering, I finished up and went to the sink to wash up. Taking time to lather up my hands, I studied my reflection in the mirror. The left side of my face was so swollen from the wasp attacks that it looked like I'd gone ten rounds with a champion boxer. I winced as I splashed water on my lesions, the coolness almost burning like I was being stung all over again.

That looks terrible, said the voice. My own voice, in a low, harsh murmur like a masked man, trying to conceal his true identity. *I'm right behind you, in the shadows,* he said. I whirled around to face the huge empty bathroom. Without warning, the fluorescent light flickered out and stayed out for a few seconds. The only remaining sounds in the darkness were the steady drips of the tap water and my forced, heavy breathing.

"Wh—who's there?" I asked, my shaky voice echoing lightly off the dingy bathroom walls.

Then the light came back on and stayed on without flickering, while my heart carried on skipping beats. I continued staring at the void until my breathing normalized. I collected myself, exited the bathroom, and rushed from the room, not bothering to look behind me. I didn't want to see whoever had spoken with my own voice.

MRS. GRIM TOOK IT EASY on me for a few days while I healed up, but I had not dared forget, or let slide, all of what Meredith had told me while I lay helpless in that hospital bed. Sheer anger began piling up in my afflicted conscience like a large dam reservoir. A very poorly constructed dam.

Mr. Grim had decided to grace us with his presence. We were all sitting together in Mrs. Grim's dining room, eating supper on the large rectangular table. I often wondered why she owned such an expensive dining table. She never had any guests over. But this evening was different. Mr. Grim's face was pale, and his fine, expensive suit had deep wrinkles all over it, hanging off his frail frame. Black rings encircled his eyes, giving him the appearance of a walking skeleton with his already emaciated physique. He looked truly a mess.

I sat quietly on my side of the table, taking out my resentment by mindlessly cutting up an especially tough piece of beef. I cut in too hard and emitted a loud clink as the tip of the knife scraped on Mrs. Grim's precious china. Both Mr. and Mrs. Grim looked up at me from their plates like spooked animals. I was an unwanted intruder in their domicile. I felt like I was being condemned to the depths of hell just by the way they stared at me.

"Sorry," I uttered. Meredith was staring too, only she looked scared, not hateful.

Mr. and Mrs. Grim both glared for an uncomfortable amount of time before grumbling and returning to their meals.

That evening dinner was by far the most uncomfortable. All I could perceive from my end of the table was the scraping of utensils on plates and the eternal howling of the wind crashing tree branches against the house. For nearly the entire sitting, Mr. and Mrs. Grim hardly conversed with one another, but they shot each other strange, conspiratorial glances.

"You two may be excused for the night. There will be no chores for either of you this evening. Now go on to your rooms, please," said Mrs. Grim. I was surprised to hear her use the word "please."

Meredith and I looked at each other, confused. Mrs. Grim had said rooms, not room.

Catching our unspoken question, Mr. Grim said, "Meredith, you will now be staying in the end chamber," Mrs Grim added. "It is no longer off limits. Now get a move on." Her tone of voice had reverted back to its typical state of crossness.

Meredith and I shot out of our chairs and ran toward the central staircase like animals heading for the safety of their dens. I waited until we were at the top of the staircase before saying to Meredith, "I saw a desk in your new room when I went in there ... that one time. Maybe there's some paper in there?"

"Oh? Wanna come have a look?" Meredith asked, waving for me to follow her. I hesitated, but she said, "Why are you taking your sweet-ass time, little brother? Just get in there." Meredith playfully pushed me aside and crossed over the threshold, me hard at her heels. She hit the power switch, and the room was immediately as bright as day.

The room's layout was different than it had been when I had stolen my way inside just a few days earlier. There was a furry rug in the centre of the room for added comfort. The lifeless cold was still present but not as extreme as before. And then I noticed that the huge mirror was gone.

"Not bad!" said Meredith, clearly excited to have her own room.

"Yeah. Looks the exact same as your old room," I teased.

Meredith wrinkled her nose and stuck out her tongue. I felt the tension leave my shoulders at her friendly teasing.

"Today's your lucky day. There's a writing pad on my new desk. Have at 'er, little brother," she said.

I tore out a few sheets from Meredith's brand-new writing pad. "Thanks," I said.

"No, just take the whole thing." Meredith smiled at me and continued examining her new room like a tourist in a lavish hotel room, her thin fingers caressing what looked like newly installed window blinds and fresh paint on the walls.

I watched her for a moment, smiling. "I'm gonna go and get a start on writing a story I have been thinking about."

"Okay. See you soon, little brother," she said. "Hey! Look at this! I even got my own walk-in wardrobe." She was about to reach for the doorknob when a flash of red light flared across my vision. That had never happened before. Ever.

"Wait," I shouted. "Don't."

"Don't what?" I was too late. Her hand had already touched the silver door handle and twisted. "Aww, it's locked."

"Probably for good reason," I whispered, my heart trying to gallop right out of my ribcage.

"Maybe," she said and moved on to examine her new bedding.

I didn't know what it was that waited for us on the other side of that closet door, but I was overwhelmed with relief. "Well, good night, sis." As she mumbled and answered, I left the room and shut the door behind me.

My mind was bursting with ideas I was dying to write down. To a certain degree, I had trouble with words and how to place them on paper due to my lack of schooling, but I managed with an old dictionary I had found in the bookshelf and the pink eraser on the back end of my pencil.

I lost track of time and didn't really know what hour it was. In the confines of my bedroom, I had no clock or watch, as Mrs. Grim forbade it. I figured it was too late to visit Meredith to say goodnight, but I heard a creak on the stairs, so I got up from my bed and poked my head into the hall.

The house was eerily silent.

Mrs. Grim had an old television,

but she wasn't a fan of it, favouring radio

and old church music records instead.

No sounds but the ticking of the old grandfather clock at the bottom of the staircase, the only clock in the house. I tiptoed down the long, narrow corridor and saw that although I had closed it after myself a few hours before, Meredith's door was slightly ajar. There was no light seeping out of the room into the hall, but I still wanted to say goodnight. I pushed the door slowly open and stepped in. It felt cold again, as cold as it had been the first time I had sneaked in there. Gooseflesh popped up all over my bare forearms.

"Meredith?" I whispered. No reply. I wanted to flick the light on but opted not to. She'd had some kind of injury as a little kid that made her breathe loudly as she slept, and I could hear her deep breathing from the bed; she was soundly asleep. There was no need for me to rudely wake her on her first night in the new room. "Goodnight again, sis," I whispered as I pulled the door closed behind me.

Taking the time to walk silently back to my room, I realized I was up later than I'd intended to be. The house was eerily silent. Mrs. Grim had an old television, but she wasn't a fan of it, favouring radio and old church music records instead. That night, there weren't any sounds of talking or praying or archaic music from the main level. I finished tiptoeing back to my room and got into bed.

I WOKE UP FEELING WELL RESTED. I rolled out of bed and was ready to start my Saturday. I was eager to see how my sister had slept on her first night in her own bed-room. Like a light-footed rabbit, I dashed to her door and pushed my way inside. The room was still dark. She must have drawn her window blinds to prevent the early morning sun from waking her up, I thought.

"Meredith," I whispered, "time to wake up. It's Saturday; let's catch some early morning cartoons before it gets too late." I tiptoed farther inside and stood beside her bed, waiting for her to shift sleepily.

I didn't even hear her usual noisy breathing.

I began feeling a rising state of distress. I broke out in a cold sweat, despite the chill in the room, and there was a heaviness in my stomach.

My knees were weak, but I managed to dash to the light switch to flick it on. Nothing happened. Now I was straight-up scared. I bolted across the creaky wooden floor and tore the heavy window blinds from their hooks. The blinds made a loud ripping sound as they crumbled to the floor in a crinkled heap.

I ran back to the side of Meredith's bed and shook her by the shoulders, not caring if she woke up and started yelling at me. No response. I placed my hand on her forehead. She was stone cold.

"Meredith!" I hollered. Sobs began to rise in my throat.

"Wake up!" I screamed over and over until my throat burned. I screamed so loud and for so long, I wouldn't have been surprised if the window broke.

"What in the Heavenly Father's name is going on in h—" Mrs. Grim burst through the door holding a small flashlight. She took one look at Meredith and stopped dead in her tracks.

As the flashlight's beam lit Meredith's face, my screams and sobs stuck in my throat. Her eyes were wide open, and her mouth gaped in a twisted, soundless scream.

"What have you done, boy?" growled Mrs. Grim.

"Nothing!" I cried, "I only just came inside to wake her up ... and now she's dead!"

MR. GRIM STUCK AROUND for only a few days after Meredith's untimely death. Mostly just to keep the atmosphere steady while the police and detectives investigated. Even though it wasn't Mrs. Grim who actually killed Meredith, I still believe they both had something to do with it.

Or at least, I thought, the bedroom did. I could feel there was an evil manifestation lurking inside that room past the midnight hour.

One cold night when the dust of suspicion began to settle, the three of us sat in the dining room having dinner. The investigating detectives had just left. I stared blankly at my plate of food. I didn't have much of an appetite, so I excused myself from dinner.

"You may go right to your bedroom, mijo," said Mrs. Grim in an eerily calm voice, devoid of emotion. She was clearly upset at the police presence having been there.

I left the dining room in a haste and marched up the stairs with a fire of hatred burning in my anguished heart.

My afflicted mentality full of animosity and despair, I stood stock still outside Meredith's empty bedroom, my mind alive with memories of her jubilant laughter and of us playing hide-and-go-seek in that huge Victorian house. Poor, sweet Meredith, my only sister. Now she was somewhere—just not there with me. I wasn't a young man of faith, despite Mrs. Grim's best efforts, but I knew wherever Meredith was, it was without a doubt better than the Grims' House of Death.

Finally, after minutes of mind tinkering, I thrust the door open with a heavy shove. My heart and soul carried an acerbic hatred for that room for killing my sister. I hated that house. I hated Mrs. Grim.

As the door swung inward, I stepped foot inside.

One step.

Two.

Three

Four.

In slow steps, I made my way into the dark, empty room. The biting cold nipped at my sleeveless arms.

The mirror.

For a reason I was unaware of, the only thought that came to mind was the creepy mirror that had been in the room before Meredith had moved in. It was back, hanging on the door of the locked closet. I moved toward the centre of the room, where I could just barely see the reflection of the central hall's chandelier illumination trickling in and dimly lighting a small portion of the darkened chamber.

Just as I suspected. Someone had moved the old mirror back in. Feeling increasingly irate, I positioned myself in front of the looking glass and deliberated over my backlit silhouette. Despite the dark, I could see I was smiling. I saw an ominous, hate-filled grin reflected in that mirror, but I knew I wasn't smiling. So, who was I looking at?

Burn this place down. Do it for her. She deserves it, does she not? It was my voice, but it sounded off, like an older me—an angrier me.

"Maybe I will," I said, leering back at my dark reflection in the huge mirror. A smile finally creased my lips.

EMERGENCY SIRENS BLARED, wailing like screaming children, along with fire engine horns trumpeting into the night. The magnificence of this fire purged the desperation of my hopeless existence. I stood tall and stared in awe at the flames dancing against the moonless, pitch-black skyline.

It was easy to fabricate a bogus story to the police and investigators, and afterwards, the social services workers. I told them that I had woken just in time to get myself safely clear of the burning house. Poor Mr. and Mrs. Grim weren't so lucky. Who wouldn't believe the words of a frightened boy, right? I was, in due course, informed by the social services case workers, with their cheap suits and solemn expressions, that I was twelve years old. I had thought I was still eleven.

After the Grims were burned to crisps, I was sent off to a boarding school for boys. As a pre-teen, no one in the foster system jumped at the opportunity to take me in. For the fourth time in my young life, I was in a hopeless situation.

It was at the school for boys where I eventually learned to fight. And quite well, might I add. Daily, I was forced into one-on-one matches over scraps of food or fending off the many adolescent sexual predators. Our incompetent headmaster ran the place like a military school. Perhaps he was ex-military—dishonorably discharged—for who in their right mind would ever want to govern such a place? With his day-by-day bouts of anger, he reminded me of my own father. Too bad this reminder wasn't heartwarming; it was terrifying.

I spent two years at the all-boys school. Two years of memories I would rather die than dredge up. It was a miracle that I was finally taken in by a Blackfoot family. Relief replaced grief because they treated me like an actual human being. I was once again back in the city of my birth, and at last with my own People.

The Willows family had never had kids of their own. My new mother, Mrs. Willows, was an instructor at one of the city's universities. Mr. Willows owned a successful renovation company. They did very well for themselves and even owned a large house on the outer rim of the sprawling suburbs.

Education was key, so I spent almost a year doing one-on-ones with Mrs. Willows, carrying out homeschooling. We had our lessons in their light-filled, comfortable lower level, which was very different from the Grims' dungeon of horrors. Mrs. Willows was very smart and had earned her master's degree in education; she told me that teaching me was an enjoyable challenge for her. The Willows even let me take their surname as my own. I was in true appreciation of my new life.

After a year, I was finally ready for real school—high school. Or so Ms. Willows thought. On my first day, I was involved in a fight with some cocky blonde kid in a black and white letter jacket—a varsity football player. My experiences in the all-boys school and a well-positioned palm to the nose instantly floored that guy.

I was suspended on my first day.

Once I was allowed back in school, it didn't take me long to become one of the misfits. Rather than spend my time cruising down the hallways with my head down as an outcast, I was welcomed into the misfit's clique. We called ourselves The Underdogs. A fitting title. None of us really fit in with other groups, and so we looked out for one another.

That's when I met Mary. Mary was from Northern Ireland and moved to Canada with her parents to escape the civil unrest running rampant over there. The other students called her "Scary Mary," but I didn't find anything scary about her. I found her enticing. She was beautiful and alluring in every way possible. She was short and curvy. Her dyed black hair tangled in messy lopsided strands over her mesmerizing, bright green eyes—if they weren't concealed by dark purple contact lenses. Mary only ever wore black. Her all-black ensembles really brought out her flawless, milky-white skin. Before me, she had only ever read about my people in textbooks. She called me an "exotic and handsome First Nations man."

Mary also introduced me to the intense sounds of Heavy Metal and Dubstep. External music had been strictly forbidden in Mrs. Grim's House of Death. I was stupefied by the brash guitars and hard-hitting drumbeats, which seemed to awaken latent senses in my mind and body.

Mary was also my first real kiss. She would be the only girl I would ever love besides my late sister, Meredith.

The high school year wore on, and we agreed to join the Underdogs at a welcome-all house party. That party was when I tasted my first enjoyable sip of alcohol—excluding the shanty town grape juice. I had a little too much vodka to drink at that party, and I blacked out. I don't remember a single thing. Weeks later, on a sunny day in May, Mary and I were taking a detour on our way home from school. She wanted to show me a secret spot down in a wilderness area she discovered. She led me to a large, concrete storm drain at the mouth of the river. We positioned ourselves on the lip of the cavern-like concrete overlooking the swiftly moving river.

I questioned her how I was when wasted off my ass at the party.

"Mmm, it was like I was seeing another side of you, a dark side. It was sexy," Mary whispered seductively into my ear. The tone in her voice turned me on straightaway. She lost her virginity that evening on the banks of that whooshing river.

The times went on. Good times. I didn't want to lose my good standing nature with the Willows family, so I kept up a steady stride of decent school grades. Mary was very smart, and she even became my one and only study partner. She agreed to tutor me, and Mrs. Willows grew fond of her.

Mary and I were finishing up homework together one Friday night, with nothing to do afterwards. She was showing off her newly dyed hair of dark lavender and her new lingerie. She looked absolutely gorgeous in her corset, with her hair spilling out of a messy bun.

"There's a huge party tonight. The squad is going. Should we go?" asked Mary, sitting cross-legged on my carpeted floor. Shared agreements are what kept our relationship strong. She stared intensely at me with bright green eyes, which seemed to sparkle like a spectral ocean in the illumination of the blue lava lamp.

"Okay. But I don't think I should drink vodka again," I answered.

"Why not?"

"I think I blacked out last time—no, I know I blacked out. And I don't really like the idea of me not remembering my good nights with you."

Trust me when I say I've seen the worst of the worst

in people when indulged in too much alcohol.

Especially in my childhood days."

She snickered. "You actually don't remember anything?"

"Not a thing. What'd I do?" I asked.

"You were like ... hmm, talking wicked. And it sort of got me wet—no, it did get me wet," she stated with a sensual flutter of her eyebrows, which made me chuckle.

"But no, for real. Please do explain." I had to inquire more because I didn't know if she was teasing or being serious. All too well, I knew she was into the whole dark arts and whatnot. But still, I needed to know if I had crossed any boundaries between us.

"I dunno. You were like a different you," she said, staring off into space, "but I'm pretty sure that's what happens to all of us when we've had too much to drink. Especially with vodka, right?"

I thought hard and long about her statement. "Did I scare you, though?"

"No way, babe. If anything, you turned me on—like to the max," she confirmed with an erotic wink. She truly had a fondness for anything to do with the darker side of existence.

"Okay, good. Trust me when I say I've seen the worst of the worst in people when indulged in too much alcohol. Especially in my childhood days."

"Your birth dad?"

I bowed my head, feeling the shame of what alcohol had done to my family so early in my young life. "Yeah."

"Aww, come here, babe." She scrambled to her feet and lunged at me, thrusting her arms around my neck and shoulders as she pressed our bodies together tightly. "Trust me, my love," she whispered into my reddening ears. "You're never going to end up like your dad. I can promise you that."

I raised my head and gazed into her green eyes. "Thank you," I said with a smile that I truly meant. My heart felt the spark of warmth that I assumed would never come. I truly loved Mary—a feeling I never thought possible after Meredith died.

CARS WERE HAPHAZARDLY PARKED for blocks, lining both sides of the treed, fence-less, neighbourhood streets. It was easy to tell which vehicles were there for the party and which were actual residents by the way they were parked. Fancy car and SUV cabins were cloaked in midnight black with people's cellphone illuminated faces inside, drinking and smoking unknown essences. The waft of weed vapours gave away their illicit doings.

"Mmmm, I love that smell," said Mary, her nose to the air as she tugged me gently forward by the hand.

Hesitantly, I kept pace with her excited, brisk walking. "Holy. Gonna be a huge party," I said, craning my neck to see further down the gentle incline of the mansion-strewn block. As we got closer to the gathering, clustered laughter of party-goers and music hung in the humid, orange glow of the night.

"Tony and Jessica just texted. Said they're already inside." Mary looked at me excitedly from checking her phone. "It's packed to the brim, and there's even a DJ and a pool." She let out a small chirpy scream while picking up her pace and tugging me along with her. I nodded nervously and kept walking. I wasn't too keen on large crowds, especially the kind full of people I didn't know.

At last, we stopped in front of the house, the address posted in bright lettering on a handmade sign. Not that it was needed; party hordes and thumping electronic music welcomed us like trumpeting courtiers.

The house was massive, with an exotic-looking, crescent-shaped driveway and large bay windows I'd only ever seen in movies and famous people magazines. Strobe lights and alternating rainbow lamps pulsed from inside the enormous house. More cars were chaotically parked on the driveway and some even on the perfectly trimmed grass. The groundskeeper would surely be upset. A large, double door entrance was wide open, with people spilling drunkenly outside and others wedging their way in.

We squeezed our way inside and started looking for our friends.

"Hey, hey. You guys made it." I recognized Tony's voice cutting through the music and indiscernible conversations. He had to push his way through a herd of new arrivals trying to find a place to hang their jackets. Low-hanging eyelids indicated that Tony was already more than a few beers deep. Straightaway he handed me an open cold one. I slugged back a huge gulp. Jessica was trailing behind on Tony's heels. She and Mary screamed when they caught sight of each other, immediately running and slamming against one another in a friendly embrace as if they hadn't just been at school together that afternoon. They were best friends. Jessica was also a metalhead, but her taste was less gothic, and she included purple or pink in her otherwise black outfits. She was just as beautiful as Mary, with long, wavy hair dyed jet-black and freckle-dotted snow-white skin.

"Come on, you guys, they're doing shots over here. Redbull and Jager." Jessica waved us over to follow her through a dense crowd of people drunkenly chatting with each other, sitting on stairs and cleared-out coffee tables. Tony followed suit, carving his way through the crowd with his beer held high above his head.

I waited for a moment until Mary spun and looked at me. A radiant smile bloomed on her purple-painted lips. Absolutely sexy. "Come, let's follow them, babe." I held her hand tight, and we set out following Tony, criss-crossing the paths of other people trying to shift their way across the tightly packed hallway.

Politely bulldozing through the masses, we finally made it past the rush-hour-like traffic of the narrow corridor and entered a big kitchen. Right away, I saw Jessica standing at a marble-topped island counter with a few of the Underdogs and some unknown partygoers. She was too occupied to see us, waving a square green bottle around and speaking at full volume to another friend.

"Let's have a shot," said Mary. "It's not vodka."

"Okay. But just one."

"Two. Please. For me?" She puckered her lips and

squinted her eyes. She knew I was a sucker for that cute look.

"Fine then. But just two. Then I'm sticking to beer after that," I asserted, waving my half-polished bottle. Mary concurred with a nimble scream and joined Jessica, already filling up a round of shot glasses.

Within a stretch of only a few minutes, The Underdogs had downed about five or six shots each of the mixed drink. The infusion of Jager and Redbull went down pretty fast. Mary giggled as she upturned an empty bottle to her lips.

We had not yet decided what was next when along came someone from a different high school, the euphoric senior brandishing capsules filled with incredibly potent molly, a popular handle for MDMA. I was a little far gone to reason, and without first weighing the potential consequences, I grabbed a tab and tossed it to the back of my mouth, followed by another shot from a random bottle of liquor lying about on the granite countertop. The rest of the squad followed suit and did the same.

I don't know how long it took for the molly to take full effect. The air of good times had a too strong a grasp on me to care about anything else. Nothing else mattered. I only remember the multiple times my lips had sealed with the soft raspberry-scented lips of my beloved Mary. The squad had turned the kitchen into our own personal VIP dance floor, our above-the-cloud bodies moving to the music like slithering snakes.

Finally, a song that my friend had shown me blasted through the DJ's huge speakers. It was a gritty synthesizer track with a mean bass line and rapid, booming beat. I remember that part as clear as day because that was the precise moment the molly's high peaked. My inner nerves seemed to be levitating serenely above the outer layer of my skin. My mood flowing like a rapid river to full, relaxed mode. Too relaxed.

I felt like I had to sit down and stay down, but of course, Mary wouldn't let me. We floated through the swaying hordes of intoxicated people and overtook the floor. The improvised dance floor in front of the DJ was being clouted by a rainbow of lasers and lightning flashes. Mary grasped me by my sweaty hands and pressed her body erotically on mine as we danced to that energetic song. I was in a state of ecstasy—another name for the drug we were high on.

The good times were flowing like wild rivers. But I had done the worst and did what I really should not have. Mixing booze and molly was not a good idea.

Once again, I unintentionally slipped into a blackout.

ALAS, I CAME TO, completely oblivious to where I was, like waking from a bad dream I already couldn't remember. My hands were scorched and smeared with what looked like blood. I felt no pain so figured the blood wasn't mine. Streaks of scarlet covered my clothes from head to toe.

I was standing in the middle of a circular, second-storey balcony. No music was playing. I could hear what sounded like people running around screaming. Their voices shrouded in terror, not delight. Fearing something terrible and shadowy had happened while my hippocampus was partly shut down, I stumbled to the balcony railing and peered over the edge. The floodlit pool was surrounded by magnificent flowers and lavish tiling. I felt my galloping heart drop to the pit of my stomach at the sight of a lone body floating face down in the pool.

If the all-black ensemble the body wore was a nail in my mind, the dark lavender hair feathering out around its head was the hammer that pounded it in. My beloved Mary. Her purple hair was floating serenely in the water around her head. A cloud of diluted blood blossomed out into the water around her sodden body.

Smashed party lights still flickered and pulsated among an array of smashed glass and strewn yard furniture while the distant wails of emergency sirens circled and closed in like a large noose, slowly clasping shut. In a matter of minutes, the loud screams and cries of people were overpowered by the whirring of helicopter motors and an army of sirens blaring in the night air.

Utterly shocked by what I saw, I stood upright and motionless, frozen on that balcony, staring down at the now-cleared-out party, not knowing that a team of tactical police officers had stealthily stormed the house. I jumped when they burst through the balcony doors, six daunting assault rifle barrels pointed my way. I couldn't for the life of me understand why this squad of heavily armed police officers were screaming at me to get on the floor, their beams of green lasers and tactical flashlights blinding me.

***

"I WOULD LIKE TO HAVE SOME WATER NOW, if that's okay with you?" Lucas asked calmly.

"Just water, okay?" Dr. Santos said, her eyes firmly affixed on her patient while she reached for the bottle she'd put back in her lab coat pocket.

"Yeah, by all means." Lucas took the bottle, uncapped it, and knocked back half of its contents in one gulp.

The Edge of Darkness

"Okay, are you ready to carry on with your story?" she asked.

"I feel pretty tired. Can we finish this tomorrow?"

"Okay," she sighed, removing her glasses and rubbing the bridge of her nose with two fingers. "But first, please, if you could at least tell me ... do you remember why you had blood on your hands and clothes?"

"I'm sorry, but I don't. Like I said: I blacked out."

"Alright. How about this?" She opened up a file folder and pressed a newspaper clipping on the glossy steel table across from Lucas. "You don't remember that at all?" she demanded, skating the clipping heatedly toward him with her index finger.

He read aloud the bold black and white headline: "Teenager brutally slain at house party." He rolled his eyes before looking inquisitively at the young doctor. "They think that was me?"

Dr. Santos nodded. "Yes, Lucas. You can't just tell me you blacked out. You have to remember something—anything." The words sputtered out from her quivering voice indicated a growing impatience about to burst.

"Nope, sorry. Can I go to bed now?"

"I'd like you to at least try and remember," she said, exasperated. "If you could just take a moment and try really hard. Please."

Lucas considered Dr. Santos for a moment. He wondered why such a beautiful woman would want to be stuck working in such a place like this. And with such people like himself.

"How about ... NO!" he screamed, snatching up the half-full water bottle and whipping it at her. It flew across the table and hit Dr. Santos in the face, knocking her glasses to the floor.

Almost instantaneously, the small, padded room was swarmed by male orderlies, all wearing the same bland blue scrubs. The last of the bulky men to enter the room pushed a cart full of vials, syringes, and anaesthetics. Lucas put up a stiff fight, kicking at the grappling orderlies and cart, right up until one of the orderlies managed to inject him with one of the syringes. His eyes slowly closed as the anesthetic took a hold of him.

As he lost consciousness, Lucas thought he heard Dr. Santos say something about getting to the bottom of a house fire. But it made no sense, and his thoughts drifted to dreams.

He woke in his dull grey room, that was more of a prison cell than a dorm room since it was always locked up. Aching and groaning, he rolled off of his stiff mattress and peered out the thin slit of a window at the pallid white yard. Another February snowstorm had settled in.

His bladder was aching to be drained.

He dashed for the shared bathroom and did his business. Staring down at the swirls of flushing water, he felt the cobwebby, heavy effects of the anesthetic they shot him full of. He needed water desperately. He cupped a few handfuls of tap water at the basin and let the cool liquid embrace his parched throat while he studied his reflection in the polished steel mirror.

Did you get it? whispered the voice.

"I did," Lucas answered sharply.

Let us see it, then.

He fished into the secret pocket that he stitched in using contraband needles and thread in the weeks past and carefully pulled out two small bottles with a clear liquid sloshing inside.

Is it what we need?

Lucas stared at the shadow behind his reflection. A malicious grin crossed his lips. "Yes. Though I was only able to get rubbing alcohol—but it's still alcohol. Just what we need."

Ahh, yes. But let us wait until tomorrow. We'll begin first with Dr. Santos. Then from there, the world is ours.

"But I kinda like Dr.—"

Am I in charge or am I not!? the voice growled.

Lucas flinched. "Yes, sorry. You're in charge."

Good. Now get some sleep. Tomorrow will be a very exciting day.

ACKNOWLEDGMENTS

FIRST OF ALL I must give a big thank you to Creator for giving me life and for giving me all the people in my life that encourage me in any way. I will forever cherish you. To the love of my life, Mary-Grace Pableo, for all the love and support she's given me from day one of our relationship. To the Tripod, Crystal Many Fingers, my mom (for all her ceaseless financial and caring love), and Patricia Soop (my sister and amazing illustrator), the other two mounts that keep my life's platform levelled out and always on top. Stepdad, Barry (Pops) who has been like a real father figure in my life.

To my publisher and editors; Lorene Shyba, Raymond Yakeleya, and Jillian Bell for all their tireless work on my manuscripts. I will never forget the support and chance you have given me. To the numerous friends and family members who have read some of my earlier works and told me to keep going; Cobie Soop, Queenie Tailfeathers, Gavin Johnston, Shane Hoof, Mike Pineda. I can also never forget my first real fans; you know who you are. Thank you everyone who has ever said anything good about my writings.

229

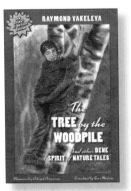
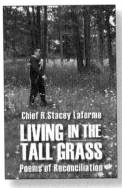

DURVILE & UpRoute Books

Other books in the

SPIRIT OF NATURE SERIES

VISIT DURVILE.COM
OR CLICK THE QR CODE FOR
MORE INFO ON THESE TITLES

SIKSIKAITSITAPI: STORIES
OF THE **BLACKFOOT PEOPLE**
By Payne Many Guns *et al*
ISBN: 9781988824833

WHY ARE YOU STILL
HERE?: A LILLIAN MYSTERY
By Lynda Partridge
ISBN: 9781988824826

NAHGANNE TALES OF THE
NORTHERN SASQUATCH
By Red Grossinger
ISBN 9781988824598

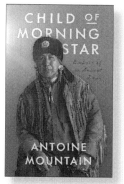

CHILD OF MORNING STAR
EMBERS OF AN **ANCIENT DAWN**
By Antoine Mountain
ISBN: 9781990735103

THE RAINBOW, THE
SONGBIRD & THE MIDWIFE
By Raymond Yakeleya
ISBN: 9781988824574

WHISTLE AT NIGHT AND
THEY WILL COME
By Alex Soop
ISBN: 9781990735301

The lands where our studios stand are a part of the ancient homeland and traditional territory of many Indigenous Nations, as places of hunting, travel, trade, and healing. The Treaty 7 Peoples of Southern Alberta include the Siksika, Piikani, and Kainai of the Niisitapi (Blackfoot) Confederacy; the Dene Tsuut'ina; and the Chiniki, Bearspaw, and Wesley Stoney Nakoda First Nations. We also acknowledge the homeland of the Métis Nation of Alberta. We honour the Nations and Peoples, as well as the land. We commit to serving the needs of Indigenous Peoples today and into the future.

ABOUT ALEX SOOP

ALEX SOOP of the Blackfoot Confederacy authentically voices his stories from First Nations Peoples' perspective. While striving to entertain with his bloodcurdling tales, Alex also integrates issues that plague Indigenous Peoples of North America. These specific issues include alcohol and drug abuse, systemic racism, missing and murdered Indigenous women and girls, foster care, suicide, residential school after-effects, and over-incarceration. He also deals with legends from Indigenous folklore, such as Wendigo, ghostly spirits, and the afterlife. His urban home is Calgary and his ancestral home is the Kainai (Blood) Nation of southern Alberta.

PHOTO: DIMA GULPA